Ratburger

Also by David Walliams:

The Boy in the Dress
Mr Stink
Billionaire Boy
Gangsta Granny
Ratburger
Demon Dentist
Awful Auntie

Both *Ratburger* and *Demon Dentist*
won the National Book Awards
Children's Book of the Year

David Walliams

Ratburger

Illustrated by Tony Ross

HarperCollins *Children's Books*

First published in hardback in Great Britain
by HarperCollins *Children's Books* 2012
HarperCollins *Children's Books* is a division of HarperCollins*Publishers* Ltd
77–85 Fulham Palace Road, Hammersmith, London W6 8JB

The HarperCollins website address is
www.harpercollins.co.uk

2

Text © David Walliams 2012
Illustrations © Tony Ross 2012

David Walliams and Tony Ross assert the moral right to be
identified as the author and illustrator of this work.

ISBN 978-0-00-792879-8

Printed and bound in England by
Clays Ltd, St Ives plc

MIX
Paper from
responsible sources
FSC
www.fsc.org
FSC C007454

FSC™ is a non-profit international organisation established to promote
the responsible management of the world's forests. Products carrying the
FSC label are independently certified to assure consumers that they come
from forests that are managed to meet the social, economic and
ecological needs of present and future generations,
and other controlled sources.

Find out more about HarperCollins and the environment at
www.harpercollins.co.uk/green

For Frankie, the boy with the beautiful smile.

Thank yous:

I would like to thank the following people, in order of importance:

Ann-Janine Murtagh, my boss at HarperCollins. I love you, I adore you. Thank you so much for believing in me, but most of all, thank you for being you.

Nick Lake, my editor. You know I think you are the absolute best in the business, but also thank you so much for helping me NOT ONLY grow as a writer, but also as a man.

Paul Stevens, my literary agent. I wouldn't pay you 10% plus VAT for making a few phone calls if I didn't feel completely blessed to be represented by you.

Tony Ross. You are the most talented illustrator in the price range we had available. Thank you.

James Stevens and Elorine Grant, the designers. Thanks.

Lily Morgan, the copy editor. Cheers.

Sam White, the publicity manager. Geraldine Stroud, the publicity director. Ta.

Meet the characters in this story:

Dad, a dad

Burt, a burger-van man

Zoe, a little girl

Sheila,
Zoe's stepmother

Mr Grave, the
headmaster

Miss Midge,
a small
teacher

Raj, a large
newsagent

Tina Trotts,
the local bully

Gingernut,
a dead
hamster

Armitage,
a live rat

1

Prawn-Cocktail-Crisp Breath

The hamster was dead.

On his back.

Legs in the air.

Dead.

With tears running down her cheeks, Zoe opened the cage. Her hands were shaking and her heart was breaking. As she laid Gingernut's little furry body down on the worn carpet, she thought she would never smile again.

"Sheila!" called Zoe, as loudly as she could. Despite her father's repeated pleas, Zoe refused to call her stepmother 'Mum'. She never had, and she vowed to herself that she never would. No one could replace Zoe's mum – not that her stepmother ever even tried.

"Shut ya face. I'm watchin' TV and stuffin' meself!" came the woman's gruff voice from the lounge.

"It's Gingernut!" called Zoe. "He's not well!"

This was an understatement.

Zoe had once seen a hospital drama on the telly where a nurse tried to revive a dying old man, so she desperately attempted to give her hamster mouth-to-mouth resuscitation by blowing very gently into his open mouth. That didn't work. Neither did connecting the rodent's little heart to an AA battery with a paper clip. It was just too late.

The hamster was cold to the touch, and he was stiff.

"Sheila! Please help...!" shouted the little girl.

At first Zoe's tears came silently, before she let out a gigantic cry. Finally she heard her stepmother trudge reluctantly down the hall of the little flat, which was situated high up on the 37th floor of a leaning tower block. The woman made huge effort noises whenever she had to do anything. She was so lazy she would order Zoe to pick her nose for her, though of course Zoe always said 'no'. Sheila could even let out a groan while changing channels with the TV remote.

"Eurgh, eurgh, eurgh, eurgh..." huffed Sheila as she thundered down the hall. Zoe's stepmother was quite short, but she made up for it by being as wide as she was tall.

She was, in a word, spherical.

Soon Zoe could sense the woman standing

Ratburger

in the doorway, blocking out the light from the hall like a lunar eclipse. What's more, Zoe could smell the sickly sweet aroma of prawn cocktail crisps. Her stepmother loved them. In fact, she boasted that from when she was a toddler she had refused to eat anything else, and spat any other food back in her mum's face. Zoe thought the crisps stank, and not even of prawns. Of course the woman's breath absolutely reeked of them too.

Even now, as she stood in the doorway, Zoe's stepmother was holding a packet of the noxious snack with one hand and feeding her face with the other while she surveyed the scene. As always, she was wearing a long grubby white T-shirt, black leggings and furry pink slippers. The bits of skin that were exposed were covered in tattoos. Her arms bore the names of her ex-husbands, all since crossed out:

"Oh dear," the woman spat, her mouth full of crisps. "Oh dear, oh dear, how very very sad. It's 'eartbreakin'. The poor little fing has snuffed it!" She leaned over her little stepdaughter and peered down at the dead hamster. She sprayed the carpet with half-chewed pieces of crisp as she spoke.

"Dear oh dear oh dear and all dat stuff," she added, in a tone that did not sound even remotely sad.

Just then a large piece of half-chewed crisp sprayed from Sheila's mouth on to the poor thing's little fluffy face. It was a mixture of crisps and spit[1]. Zoe wiped it away gently, as a tear dropped from her eye on to his cold pink nose.

"'Ere, I got a great idea!" said Zoe's stepmother. "I'll just finish dese crisps and ya can shove the little fing in de bag. I won't touch it meself. I don't wanna catch summink."

Sheila lifted the bag above her mouth and poured the last of the prawn cocktail crisp crumbles down her greedy throat. The woman then offered her stepdaughter the empty bag. "Dere ya go. Bung it in 'ere, quick. Before it stinks de whole flat out."

Zoe almost gasped at the unfairness of what the woman had just said. It was her fat stepmother's

---

[1] *The technical name for this is a 'spisp'.*

prawn-cocktail-crisp breath that stank the place out! Her breath could strip paint. It could shear the feathers off a bird and make it bald. If the wind changed direction, you would get a nasty waft of her breath in a town ten miles away.

"I am not burying my poor Gingernut in a crisp packet," snapped Zoe. "I don't know why I called for you in the first place. Please just go!"

"For goodness' sake, girl!" shouted the woman. "I was only trying to 'elp. Ungrateful little wretch!"

"Well, you're not helping!" shouted Zoe, without turning round. "Just go away! Please!"

Sheila thundered out of the room and slammed the door so hard that plaster fell from the ceiling.

Zoe listened as the woman she refused to call 'Mum' trudged back to the kitchen, no doubt to rip open another family-sized bag of prawn cocktail crisps to fill her face with. The little girl was left alone in her tiny bedroom, cradling her dead hamster.

But how had he died? Zoe knew that Gingernut was very young, even in hamster years.

Could this be a hamster murder? she wondered.

But what kind of person would want to murder a defenceless little hamster?

Well, before this story is over, you will know. And you will also know that there are people capable of doing much, much worse. The most evil man in the world is lurking somewhere in this very book. Read on, if you dare…

2

A Very Special Little Girl

Before we meet this deeply wicked individual, we need to go back to the beginning.

Zoe's real mum died when she was a baby, but Zoe had still had a very happy life. Dad and Zoe had always been a little team, and he showered her with love. While Zoe was at school, Dad went out to work at the local ice-cream factory. He had adored ice cream ever since he was a boy and loved working in the factory, even though his job involved long hours, not much money and very hard work.

What kept Zoe's dad going was making

brand new ice-cream flavours. At the end of every shift at the factory he would rush home excitedly, laden with samples of some weird and wonderful new flavour for Zoe to be the first to try. Then he would report back what she liked to the boss. These were Zoe's favourites:

Sherbert Bang
Bubblicious Bubblegum
Triple Choco-Nut-Fudge Swirl
Candyfloss Supreme

Caramel & Custard

Mango Surprise

Cola Cube & Jelly

Peanut Butter & Banana Foam

Pineapple & Liquorice

Whizz Fizz Spacedust Explosion

Her least favourite was Snail & Broccoli. Not even Zoe's dad could make snail and broccoli ice cream taste good.

Not all of the flavours made it to the shops (especially not Snail & Broccoli) but Zoe tried them all! Sometimes she ate so much ice cream she thought she would explode. Best of all, she would often be the only child in the world to try them, and that made Zoe feel like a very special little girl indeed.

There was one problem.

Being an only child, Zoe had no one at home

to play with, apart
from her dad, who
worked long hours
at the factory. So by
the time she reached
the age of nine, like
many kids, she
wanted a pet with
all her heart and soul.
It didn't have to be
a hamster, she just
needed something,
anything, to love.
Something that she
hoped would love
her back. However,
living on the 37th
floor of a leaning
tower block, it had

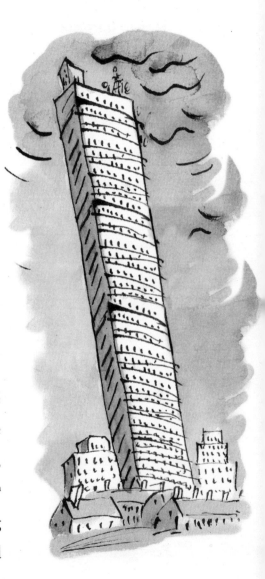

to be something small.

So, on Zoe's tenth birthday, as a surprise, Dad left work early and met his daughter at the school gates. He carried her on his shoulders – she had always loved that ever since she was a baby – and took her to the local pet shop. There, he bought her a hamster.

Zoe picked out the fluffiest, cutest baby one, and named him Gingernut.

Gingernut lived in a cage in the little girl's bedroom. Zoe didn't mind that Gingernut would go round and round on his wheel at night keeping her awake. She didn't mind that he nipped her finger a couple of times when she fed him biscuits as a special treat. She even didn't mind that his cage smelled of hamster wee.

In short, Zoe loved Gingernut. And Gingernut loved Zoe.

Zoe didn't have many friends at school.

What's more, the other kids bullied her for being short and ginger and having to wear braces on her teeth. Just one of those things would have been enough for her to have a hard time. She had hit the jackpot with all three.

Gingernut was small and ginger too, though of course he didn't wear braces. That smallness and gingerness was probably, deep down, why Zoe chose him out of the dozens of little balls of fluff snuggled up together behind the glass at the pet shop. She must have sensed a kindred spirit.

Over the weeks and months that followed, Zoe taught Gingernut some mind-boggling tricks. For a sunflower seed, he would stand on his back legs and do a little dance. For a walnut, Gingernut would do a back-flip. And for a lump of sugar, he would spin around on his back.

Zoe's dream was to make her little pet world famous as the very first breakdancing hamster!

She planned to put on a little show at Christmas for all the other children on the estate. She even made a poster to advertise it.

Gingernut
The Breakdancing hamster

he Locks   he Uprocks
he floor rocks   he does the
Robot

he is learning the Windmill
but can't quite do it yet!

ON THE DECKS - ZOE

Then one day, Dad came home from work with some very sad news, which would tear their happy little life apart...

3

Nuffink

"I lost my job," said Dad.

"No!" said Zoe.

"They are shutting down the factory – moving the whole operation to China."

"But you will find another job, won't you?"

"I will try," said Dad. "But it won't be easy. There'll be loads of us all looking for the same ones."

And as it turned out, it wasn't easy. It was, in fact, impossible. With so many people losing their jobs all at once, Dad was forced to claim benefit money from the government. It was a pittance, barely enough to live on. With nothing to do all day, Dad became more and more down. To begin with he went to the Job Centre every day. But there were never any jobs within a hundred miles and eventually he started going to the pub instead – Zoe could tell because she was fairly sure that Job Centres didn't stay open till late at night.

Zoe became more and more worried about her father. Sometimes she wondered if he had given up on life altogether. Losing first his wife, and then his job, seemed like just too much for him to bear.

Little did he know, things were about to get much much worse...

Dad met Zoe's stepmother when he was at his saddest. He was lonely and she was on her own, her last husband having died in a mysterious prawn-cocktail-crisp-related incident. Sheila seemed to think that husband number ten's benefit money would provide her with an easy life, with fags on tap and all the prawn cocktail crisps she could eat.

As Zoe's real mum had died when Zoe was a baby, as much as she tried, and she tried and tried, Zoe could not remember her. There used to be photographs of Mum up all over the flat. Mum had a kind smile. Zoe would stare at the photographs, and try and smile just like her. They certainly looked alike. Especially when they were smiling.

However, one day when everyone was out, Zoe's new stepmother took all the photographs down. Now they were conveniently 'lost'. Probably burned. Dad didn't like talking about Mum because it would just make him cry. However, she lived on in Zoe's heart. The little girl knew that her real mum had loved her very much. She just knew it.

Zoe also knew her stepmother did *not* love her. Or even like her very much. In truth, Zoe was pretty sure her stepmother hated her. Sheila treated her at worst as an irritant, at best as if she were invisible. Zoe often overheard her stepmother saying she wanted her out of the house as soon as she was old enough.

"De little brat can stop spongin' off me!" The woman never gave her a penny, not even on her birthday. That Christmas, Sheila had given Zoe a used tissue as a present, and then laughed in her face when the little girl unwrapped it. It was full of snot.

Soon after Zoe's stepmother moved into the flat, she demanded that the hamster move out.

"It stinks!" she shrieked.

However, after a great deal of shouting and slamming of doors, Zoe was finally allowed to keep her little pet.

Sheila carried on despising Gingernut, though. She moaned and moaned that the little hamster chewed holes in the sofa, even though it was burning hot ash falling from her fags that had really created them! Over and over again she warned her stepdaughter she would "stamp on de nasty little beast if I ever catch it out of its cage".

Sheila also mocked Zoe's attempts to teach her hamster to breakdance.

"You're wastin' your time with dat nonsense. You and dat little beast will amount to nuffink. Ya 'ear me? Nuffink!"

Zoe heard, but chose not to listen. She knew she had a special way with animals, and Dad had always told her so.

In fact, Zoe dreamed of travelling the world with a huge menagerie of animal stars. One day, she would train animals to do extraordinary feats that she believed would delight the world. She even made a list of what these madcap acts could be:

A frog who is a superstar DJ

A rapping terrapin

Two gerbils who ballroom dance together

An elephant who
sings opera

A donkey who does
magic tricks

A tap-dancing
centipede

A boy band comprised entirely of guinea pigs

A street-dance group of tortoises

A cat who does impressions
(of famous cartoon cats)

A ballet-dancing pig

A worm hypnotist

A high-wire acrobatics
act with cows

An ant who does
ventriloquism

A daredevil mole who does incredible stunts like being shot out of a cannon

A karate display with jellyfish

A bungee-jumping hippopotamus

Zoe had it all planned out. With the money the animals earned, she and her father could both escape the leaning, crumbling tower block for ever. Zoe could buy Dad a much bigger flat, and she could retire to a huge country house and set up a sanctuary for unwanted pets. The animals could run around in the grounds all day, and sleep together in a giant bed at night. 'No animal too big or too small, they will all be loved' was to be written over the entrance gates.

Then on that fateful day, Zoe came home from school to find that Gingernut was dead. And with him, Zoe's dreams of animal-training stardom died too.

So, reader, after that little journey back in time, we're back at the start, and ready to get on with the story.

Don't turn back to the beginning though,

that would be really stupid and you would go round and round in circles reading the same few pages. No, move on to the next page, and I will continue with the story. Quickly. Stop reading this and move on. Now!

4

Dirty Business

"Flush it down de bog!" shouted Sheila.

Zoe was sitting on her bed listening through the wall to her dad and stepmother arguing.

"No!" replied Dad.

"Give it 'ere ya useless git! I'll bung it in de bin!"

Zoe often sat on her bed in her too-small pyjamas, listening through the paper-thin wall to her father and stepmother arguing way past her bedtime. Tonight they were of course shouting and screaming about Gingernut, who had died that day.

As they lived in a flat on the 37th floor of a dilapidated council block (which leaned heavily and should have been demolished decades ago), the family didn't have a garden. There *was* an old adventure playground in the central concrete square shared by all the blocks in the estate. However, the local gang made it too dangerous to venture near.

"Wot you lookin' at?" Tina Trotts would shout at anyone passing by. Tina was the local bully, and her gang of teenage hoodlums ruled the estate. She was only fourteen but she could make a grown man cry, and often did. Every day she would flob on Zoe's head from the flats as the little girl walked to school. And every day Tina would laugh, as if it was the funniest thing in the world.

If the family had owned an allotment or even the smallest patch of grass anywhere on the estate they could call their own, Zoe would have dug a little grave with a spoon, lowered her little friend into the hole and made a headstone with a lolly stick.

> *Gingernut,*
> *Much loved Hamster,*
> *Expert breakdancer,*
> *And sometime bodypopper.*
> *Sadly missed by his owner and friend Zoe,*
> *RIP* [2]

But of course they didn't have a garden. No one did. Instead, Zoe had wrapped her hamster carefully in a page from her History exercise book. When her dad finally returned home from the pub, Zoe gave him the precious little package.

---

[2] *It would have had to be quite a big lolly stick.*

My dad will know what to do with him, she thought.

But Zoe hadn't reckoned on her horrible stepmother getting involved.

Unlike his new wife, Dad was tall and thin. If she was a bowling ball, he was the skittle, and of course bowling balls often knock over skittles.

So now Dad and Sheila were arguing in the kitchen about what to do with the little package Zoe had given to Dad. It was always awful hearing the two of them shouting at each other, but tonight was proving particularly unbearable.

"I suppose I could get the poor girl another hamster," ventured Dad. "She was so good with it…"

Zoe's face lit up for a moment.

"Are ya crazy?" sneered her stepmother. "Another 'amster! You are so useless, ya can't even get a job to pay for one!"

"There *are* no jobs," pleaded Dad.

"You're just too lazy to get one. Ya useless git."

"I could find a way, for Zoe. I love my girl so much. I could try to save up some of my benefit money—"

"Dat's hardly enuff to keep me in prawn cocktail crisps, let alone feed a beast like dat."

"We could feed it leftovers," protested Dad.

"I am not havin' another one of dose disgusting creatures in me flat!" said the woman.

"It's not a disgusting creature. It's a hamster!"

"'Amsters are no better dan rats," Sheila continued. "Worse! I work all day on me 'ands and knees keepin' dis flat spick and span."

She does no such thing, thought Zoe. *The flat is an absolute tip!*

"And den the nasty little fing comes along and does its dirty business everywhere!" continued

Sheila. "And while I am on the subject, your aim in de bog could be better!"

"Sorry."

"Wot do ya do? Put a sprinkler on de end of it?"

"Keep your voice down, woman!"

The little girl was once again finding out the hard way that secretly listening to your parents talk could be a very dangerous game. You always ended up hearing things you wished you never had. Besides, Gingernut *didn't* do his dirty business everywhere. Zoe always made sure she picked up any rogue droppings from his secret runs around her room with some loo paper and flushed them safely down the toilet.

"I'll take the cage down the pawn shop then," said Dad. "I might get a few quid for it."

"*I* will take it down de pawn shop," said his wife aggressively. "You'll just spend the money down de pub."

"But—"

"Now put de nasty little fing in de bin."

"I promised Zoe I would give him a proper burial in the park. She loved Gingernut. Taught him tricks and everything."

"Dey were pathetic. PATHETIC! A breakdancin' 'amster?! Absolute rubbish!"

"That's not fair!"

"And you're not going out again tonight. I don't trust ya. You'll be back down de pub."

"It's shut now."

"Knowing you, you'll just wait outside until it opens tomorrow morning… Now come on, give it 'ere!"

Zoe heard the pedal bin open with the stamp of her stepmother's chubby foot and the faint sound of a thud.

With tears streaming down her face, Zoe lay

down in bed, and covered herself with her duvet. She turned to her right side. In the half-light she stared at the cage as she did every night.

It was agonising to see it empty. The little girl closed her eyes but couldn't sleep. Her heart was aching, her brain was spinning. She was sad, she was angry, she was sad, she was angry, she was sad. She turned on to her left side. Maybe it would be easier to sleep facing the grimy wall rather than staring at the empty cage. She closed her eyes again, but all she could think about was Gingernut.

Not that it was easy to think, what with the noise coming from the neighbouring flat. Zoe didn't know who lived there – people in the tower block weren't exactly close – but most evenings she heard shouting. It seemed like a man screaming at his daughter, who would often cry, and Zoe felt sorry for her, whoever she was. However bad Zoe thought her life was, this girl's sounded worse.

But Zoe blocked out the shouting, and soon fell asleep, dreaming of Gingernut, breakdancing in heaven…

5

Droppings

Zoe trudged even more reluctantly than usual to school the next morning. Gingernut was dead, and with that her dreams had died too. As Zoe walked out of the estate, Tina flobbed on the little girl's head as she always did. As she was wiping the flob out of her frizzy hair with a page ripped from one of her exercise books, Zoe saw Dad crouched over by the tiniest patch of grass.

He appeared to be digging with his hands.

He turned around quickly, as if in shock. "Oh, hello, my love…"

"What are you doing?" said Zoe. She leaned

over him, to see what he was up to, and saw that the little package containing Gingernut was laid on the ground, next to a small mound of earth.

"Don't tell your mum…"

"Stepmum!"

"Don't tell your stepmum, but I fished the little fella out of the bin…"

"Oh, Dad!"

"Sheila's still asleep, snoring away. I don't think she heard anything. Gingernut meant so much to you and I just wanted to give him, you know, a proper burial."

Zoe smiled for a moment, but somehow she found herself crying too.

"Oh, Dad, thank you so much…"

"No word of this to her though, or she'll murder me."

"Of course not."

Zoe knelt down beside him, picked up the

little package and lowered Gingernut into the small hole her father had dug.

"I even got one of these for a headstone. One of the old lolly sticks from the factory."

Zoe took out her chewed biro from her pocket, and scribbled 'Gingernut' on the stick, though there wasn't really room for the 't', so it just read:

GINGERNU

Dad filled in the hole, and they stood back and looked at the little grave.

"Thanks, Dad. You are the best…"

Now Dad was crying.

"What's the matter?" asked Zoe.

"I am not the best. I am so sorry, Zoe. But I will get another job one day. I know I will…"

"Dad, a job doesn't matter. I just want you to be happy."

"I don't want you to see me like this…"

Dad started walking away. Zoe pulled on his arm, but he shook it out of her grasp, and walked off back to the tower block.

"Come and meet me at the school gates later, Dad. We can go to the park, and you can put me on your shoulders. I used to love that. It don't cost a thing."

"Sorry, I'll be in the pub. Have a good day at school," he shouted, without looking back. He was hiding his sadness from his daughter, like he always did.

Zoe could feel her stomach screaming in hunger. There had been no dinner last night as Sheila had spent all the benefit money on fags, and there was no food in the house. Zoe hadn't eaten for a very long time. So she stopped off at Raj's Newsagent.

All the kids from school went to his shop before or after school. As Zoe never received pocket money, she would only come in to the shop and gaze longingly at the sweets. Being exceptionally kind-hearted, Raj often took pity on the girl and gave her free ones. Only the out-of-date ones though, or those with a hint of mould, but she was still grateful. Sometimes she would be allowed a quick suck on a mint before Raj asked her to spit it out so he could put it back in the packet to sell it to another customer.

This morning Zoe was especially hungry, and

was hoping Raj would help…

TING went the bell as the door opened.

"Aaah! Miss Zoe. My favourite customer." Raj was a big jolly man, who always had a smile on his face, even if you told him his shop was on fire.

"Hello, Raj," said Zoe sheepishly. "I don't have any money again today I am afraid."

"Not a penny?"

"Nothing. Sorry."

"Oh dear. But you do look hungry. A quick nibble on one of these chocolate bars perhaps?"

He picked up a bar and unwrapped it for her.

"Just try and eat around the edge please. Then I can put it in the wrapper and back on sale. The next customer will never know!"

Zoe nibbled greedily on the chocolate bar, her front teeth munching off the edges like a little rodent.

"You look very sad, child," said Raj. He was always good at spotting when things were wrong, and could be a lot more caring than some parents or teachers. "Have you been crying?"

Zoe looked up from her nibbling for a moment. Her eyes still stung with tears.

"No, I'm fine, Raj. Just hungry."

"No, Miss Zoe, I can see something is wrong." He leaned on the counter, and smiled supportively at her.

Zoe took a deep breath. "My hamster died."

"Oh, Miss Zoe, I am so so sorry."

"Thank you."

"You poor thing. A few years ago I had a pet tadpole and it died, so I know how you feel."

Zoe looked surprised. "A pet tadpole?" She had never heard of anyone having one as a pet.

"Yes, I called him Poppadom. One night I left him swimming around in his little fish bowl, and when I woke up in the morning there was this naughty frog there. He must have eaten Poppadom!"

Zoe couldn't quite believe what she was hearing.

"Raj…"

"Yes…?" The newsagent wiped a tear from his eye with the sleeve of his cardigan. "Sorry, I always get quite emotional when I think about Poppadom."

"Raj, tadpoles turn into frogs."

"Don't be so stupid, child!"

"They do. So that frog *was* Poppadom."

"I know you are just making me feel better, but I know it's not true."

Zoe rolled her eyes.

"Now tell me about your hamster…"

"He is, I mean, was, so special. I trained him to breakdance."

"Wow! What was his name?"

"Gingernut," said Zoe sadly. "My dream was that one day he would be on the TV…"

Raj thought for a moment, and then looked Zoe straight in the eyes. "You must never give up on your dreams, young lady…"

"But Gingernut is dead…"

"But your *dream* doesn't need to die. Dreams never die. If you can train a hamster to breakdance, Miss Zoe, just imagine what you could do…"

"I suppose…"

Raj looked at his watch. "But as much as I would like to, we can't stand here chatting all day."

"No?" Zoe loved Raj, even if he didn't know a tadpole turned into a frog, and never wanted to leave his messy little shop.

"You better be off to school now, young lady.

You don't want to be late…"

"I suppose so," mumbled Zoe. Sometimes she wondered why she didn't just bunk off like so many of the others.

Raj beckoned with his big hands. "Now, Miss Zoe, give me the chocolate bar please, so I can put it back on sale…"

Zoe looked at her hands. It had gone. She was so hungry she had devoured every last morsel, save for one tiny square.

"I am so sorry, Raj. I didn't mean to. I really didn't!"

"I know, I know," said the kindly man. "Just put it back in the wrapper. I can sell it as a special diet chocolate to someone fat like me!"

"Good idea!" said the little girl.

Zoe went over to the door, and turned around to face the newsagent.

"Thank you, by the way. Not just for the

chocolate. But for the advice…"

"Both are free of charge for you any time, Miss Zoe. Now run along…"

Raj's words went round and round in Zoe's mind all day at school, but when she returned home to the flat she felt the same sense of absence. Gingernut was gone. For ever.

Days went by, then weeks, then months. She could never forget about Gingernut. He was such a special little hamster. And he brought her so much joy in a world of pain. From the moment he died, Zoe felt as if she was walking through a storm. Very slowly, as the days and weeks passed, the rain became a little lighter. Though the sun had still not shone.

Until one night, months later, when something completely unexpected happened.

Zoe was lying in bed after another insufferable

day at school at the hands of the bullies, and the dreaded Tina Trotts in particular. There was shouting from next door as usual. Then, out of a brief moment of quiet in the night, came a tiny sound. It was so soft at first it was almost imperceptible. Then it became louder. And louder.

It sounded like nibbling.

Am I dreaming? thought Zoe. *Am I having one of those strange dreams that I am lying in bed awake?*

She opened her eyes. No, she wasn't dreaming.

Something small was moving in her bedroom.

For a mad moment, Zoe wondered if it could be the ghost of Gingernut. Lately she'd found a couple of what seemed like droppings in her room. *No, don't be crazy*, she told herself. *Must be funny-shaped clumps of dust, that's all.*

At first all she could see was a tiny shadowy

shape in the corner by the door. She tiptoed out of bed to have a closer look. It was little and dirty and a tad smelly. The dusty floorboards creaked a little under her weight.

The tiny thing turned around.

It was a rat.

6

Rat-a-tat-tat

When you think of the word 'rat', what is the next thing to come into your head?

Rat... vermin?

Rat... sewer?

Rat... disease?

Rat... bite?

Rat... plague?

Rat... catcher?

Rat... a-tat-tat?

Rats are the most unloved living things on the planet.

Kittens

Puppies

Bunnies

Hamsters

Gerbils

Guinea pigs

Baby elephants

Koala bears

Piglets

Penguins

Butterflies

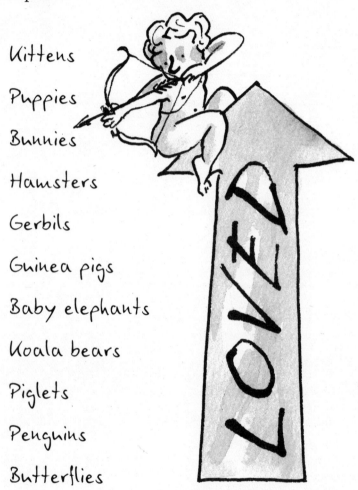

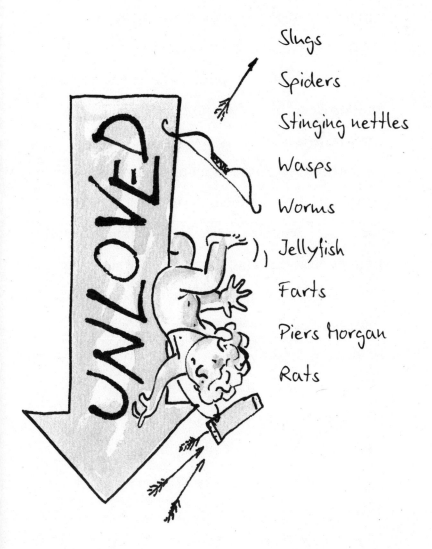

Slugs

Spiders

Stinging nettles

Wasps

Worms

Jellyfish

Farts

Piers Morgan

Rats

However, what if I told you that what Zoe found in her room that night was a *baby* rat?

Yes, this was the cutest, sweetest, littlest baby rat you can imagine, and it was crouching in the corner of her room, nibbling on one of her dirty hole-ridden socks.

With a tiny pink twitching nose, furry ears and huge, deep, hopeful eyes, this was a rat that could win first prize in a vermin beauty pageant. This explained the mysterious droppings that Zoe had recently found in her room: it must have been this little mite.

Well, it certainly wasn't me.

Zoe had always thought she would be terrified if she ever saw a rat. Her stepmother even kept rat poison in the kitchen, as there was always talk of an infestation in the crumbling block of flats.

However, this rat didn't seem very terrifying.

In fact, if anything, the rat appeared to be terrified of *Zoe*. When the floorboard creaked as she approached, it skirted the wall and hid under her bed.

"Don't be scared, little one," whispered Zoe. Slowly she put her hand under the bed to try and stroke the rat. It shivered in fear at first, its fur standing up on end.

"Shush, shush," said Zoe, comfortingly.

Little by little, the rat made its way through the garden of dust and dirt under Zoe's creaky little bed and approached her hand. It sniffed her fingers, before licking one, then another. Sheila was too idle to cook, and Zoe was so starving she had stolen a bag of her stepmother's dreaded prawn cocktail crisps for her dinner. The rat must have been able to smell them on her fingers, and despite Zoe's grave misgivings about the snack, which bore no relation to prawns or indeed cocktails, the rat didn't seem to mind.

Zoe let out a little giggle. The nibbling tickled her. She lifted her hand to stroke the rat, and it ducked underneath and raced to the far corner of the room.

"Shush, shush, come on. I only want to give you a stroke," implored Zoe.

The rat peeked at her with uncertainty, before tentatively, paw by paw, making its way over to her hand. She brushed its fur with her little finger as lightly as she could. The fur was a lot softer than she imagined. Not as soft as Gingernut's, nothing was. But surprisingly soft nonetheless.

One by one, Zoe's fingers lowered and soon she was stroking the top of the rat's head. Zoe let her fingers trickle down its neck and back. The rat arched its back to meet her hand.

Most likely it had never been shown such tenderness before. Certainly not by a human. Not only was there enough rat poison in the world to kill every rat ten times over, but when people saw a rat, they would generally either scream or reach for a broom to whack it with.

Looking at this little tiddler now, though, it was hard for Zoe to understand why anyone would want to harm him.

Suddenly, the rat's little ears shot up and Zoe quickly turned her head. Her parents' bedroom door was opening, and she could hear her stepmother thundering along the hallway, huffing with each step. Hurriedly, Zoe snatched up the rat, cupped it in her hands, and jumped back into bed. Sheila would go crazy if she knew her stepdaughter was in bed cuddling a rodent. Zoe took the duvet between her teeth and hid under the covers. She waited and listened. The bathroom door creaked open and closed, and Zoe could hear the muffled sound of her stepmother thudding down on to the cracked toilet seat.

Zoe sighed and opened her hands. The baby rat was safe. For now. She let the little rodent scamper over her hands and on to her torn pyjama top.

"Kiss kiss kiss kiss." She made a little kissing

noise just like the one she used to do with Gingernut. And just like her hamster used to do, the rat approached her face.

Zoe planted a little kiss on its nose. She pushed a dent in the pillow next to her head, and gently laid the rat down into it. It fitted perfectly, and soon she could hear it snoring very quietly next to her.

If you have never heard a rat snoring before, this is what it sounds like:

ZZZZZZZZZZZZZZZZZZZZZZZZZZZ ZZZZZZZZZZZZ zzzzzzzzzzz zzzzzzzzzzzzzzzzzz.

"Now, how on earth am I going to keep you a secret?" Zoe whispered.

7

Animal Smuggling

It isn't easy to smuggle a rat into school.

The hardest animal to sneak into school is of course the blue whale. Just too big and wet.

Hippopotamuses are also hard to slip in unnoticed, as are giraffes. Too fat and tall respectively.

Lions are inadvisable. All that roaring gives them away.

Seals bark too much. As do walruses.

Skunks smell really bad – even worse than some teachers.

Kangaroos just don't stop hopping.

Boobies[3] sound too rude.

Elephants tend to break the chairs.

An ostrich will get you to school quickly, but is too big to hide in your school bag.

Polar bears blend into arctic wastes very well, but can be spotted instantly in a school dinner queue.

Smuggling a shark into school would lead to instant expulsion, especially if you had

---

[3] *A booby is a type of seabird closely related to the gannet. In case you thought I had made it up for a cheap laugh. As if I would do that!*

swimming lessons that day. They have a tendency to eat the children.

Orang-utans are also a no-no. They can be very disruptive in class.

Gorillas are even worse, especially in Maths. Gorillas are not good with numbers, and hate doing sums, although they are surprisingly good at French.

A herd of wildebeest is almost impossible to take into school without a teacher noticing.

Nits, on the other hand, are ludicrously easy. Some children smuggle thousands of nits into school every day.

A rat is still a difficult animal to smuggle into school. Somewhere between a blue whale and a nit on the 'hard to smuggle into school' scale.

The problem was that it was impossible for Zoe to leave the little thing at home. Gingernut's old battered cage was long gone, as her stepmother had taken it to the pawnbrokers. The ghastly woman had swapped it for a few coins, which she promptly spent on a bumper-box of prawn cocktail crisps. Thirty-six bags that she had demolished before breakfast.

If Zoe had just left the rat running around the flat, she knew that Sheila would have poisoned it or stamped on it or both. Her stepmother made no secret of hating all rodents. And even if Zoe had hidden the rat in a bedroom drawer, or in a box under her bed, there was a very good chance Sheila would have found it. Zoe knew that her stepmother always rummaged through her possessions the moment she left for school. Sheila was looking for things she could sell or swap for a fag or two, or some more prawn cocktail crisps.

One day, all of Zoe's toys had gone, another day it was her beloved books. It was just too risky to leave the rat alone in the flat with that woman.

Zoe considered putting the rat in her school bag, but because she was so poor she had to take her books to school in a beaten-up plastic carrier bag, held together with strips of sticky tape. It was too much of a risk that the little rodent might nibble its way out. So Zoe hid it in the breast pocket of her two-sizes-too-large blazer. Yes, she could feel it constantly wriggling around, but at least she knew it was safe.

As Zoe came out of the stairwell of the tower block and into the concreted communal area, she heard a shout from above her. "Zoe!"

She looked up.

Big mistake.

A huge flobbet of flob flobbed square on to her face. Zoe saw Tina Trotts standing at the railings several floors up.

"HA HAH HA!" Tina shouted down.

Zoe refused to cry. She just wiped her face with her sleeve and turned away, Tina's laughter still echoing behind her. She probably *would* have cried, but then she felt the little rat move in her pocket, and she instantly felt better.

Now I've got a little pet again, she thought. *It might just be a rat, but it's only the beginning...*

Perhaps Raj was right: her dream of training an animal to entertain the nation wasn't dead after all.

The rat's presence remained a comfort when Zoe arrived at school. This was Zoe's first year at big school and she hadn't made a single friend there yet. Most of the kids were poor, but Zoe was the poorest. It was embarrassing for her to have to go to school in unwashed clothes from charity shops. Clothes which were either far too big or far too small for her, and most of which had gaping holes in them. The rubber sole had all but fallen off her left shoe, and flapped against the ground every time she took a step.

FLIP FLAP FLIP FLAP FLIP FLAP went her shoes every time she walked anywhere.

FLIPITY FLAP FLIPITY FLAP FLIPITY FLAP if she ran.

In assembly, after an announcement about an end-of-term talent show, the pale headmaster Mr Grave stepped up to speak. He stood in the centre of the stage, unblinkingly staring at the hundreds of pupils gathered in the school hall. All the children were a little bit scared of him. With his staring eyes and pale skin, wild rumours abounded among the younger pupils that he was secretly a vampire.

Mr Grave proceeded to give a stern warning to those "errant pupils" who, against the rules, had been smuggling their mobile phones into school. This was just about everyone, though Zoe was far too skint to even dream of ever owning one.

Great, thought Zoe. *Even when we're being told off I get left out.*

"Needless to say, I'm not just talking about phones!" boomed Mr Grave, as if reading Zoe's mind. His voice could carry across a crowded playground at break-time and make every pupil fall silent in a heartbeat. "*Anything* that beeps or vibrates is strictly forbidden! Did you hear me?" he boomed again.

"Forbidden! That is all. Dismissed."

The bell rang and the kids plodded off to their lessons. Sitting on the uncomfortable little grey plastic chair on her own lonely row at the back of the assembly hall, Zoe wondered nervously if her rat came under Mr Grave's description. It certainly vibrated. And sometimes it beeped. Or at least squeaked.

"Don't make a sound today, little rat," she said.

The rat squeaked.

Oh no! thought Zoe.

8

Bread Sandwich

So as not to be jostled at the door, Zoe waited a few moments before ambling off to her first lesson. Amazingly, Maths, which she always found cataclysmically boring, passed without incident. As did Geography, where she wondered if her new-found knowledge of oxbow lakes might come in useful in adult life. During the lessons, Zoe stole an occasional glance into her blazer inside pocket, and saw that the little rat was sleeping. It must really enjoy a nice lie-in.

At break-time, Zoe locked herself in a cubicle in the girls' toilets and fed the rat some of the bread she was meant to be saving for her lunch. She made her own packed lunch whenever there were scraps of food still in the house. However, this morning there was absolutely nothing in the fridge other than a few cans of very strong lager, so she made herself a bread sandwich out of some stale slices left out on the side…

The recipe was simple:

BREAD SANDWICH

You will need: *three slices of bread.*

Instructions: take one slice of bread, and put it between the other two slices of bread.

The end.[4]

---

[4] My new cookbook, *101 Ways to Make a Bread Sandwich*, is out next year.

Unsurprisingly, the rat liked bread. Rats like most food we like.

Zoe sat on the toilet seat, and the rat perched on her left hand while she fed it with her right. It gobbled up every last mouthful.

"There you go, little—"

At that moment Zoe realised she had yet to name her tiny friend. Unless she wanted to give it a name suitable for a boy or a girl like 'Pat' or

'Les' or 'Viv', she would first have to find out if it was indeed a boy or a girl. So Zoe carefully picked the rat up to have a closer look. Just as she was trying to undertake a more thorough investigation, a thin arch of yellow liquid sprayed from just underneath the rat's tummy, narrowly missing Zoe, and decorating the wall.

The girl now had a definitive answer. She was convinced that the wee had come from a tiny little spout, though it was impossible to look again, with the rat now wriggling in her hands.

But she was sure it was a boy.

Zoe looked up for inspiration. On the toilet door, some older girls had scratched obscene sentences with a compass.

'Destiny is a complete @**$$$$&!%^!%!!!!' Zoe read, which I think we can all agree is very rude, even if she is.

Destiny would have been a stupid name for

a rat. Especially a boy rat, thought the little girl. Zoe continued searching the names on the door for inspiration.

Rochelle... no.

Darius... no.

Busta... no.

Tupac... no.

Jammaall... no.

Snoop... no.

Meredith... no.

Kylie... no.

Beyonce...no.

Tyrone... no.

Chantelle... no.

Despite being crowded with words (and some rude drawings), the toilet door wasn't providing as much inspiration as Zoe had hoped. She sat up from the toilet seat and turned around to flush, so as not to alert the suspicion of the girl she could hear in the next cubicle. At that moment, she spied some posh writing amidst all the ingrained stains in the toilet bowl.

"Armitage Shanks," she read out loud. It was only the name of the toilet manufacturer, but the little rat's ears twitched when she said it, as if in recognition.

"Armitage! That's it!" she exclaimed. It was a suitably upper-class-sounding name for this special little fellow.

Suddenly there was a loud thud on the toilet door.

BOOM
BOOOM
BOOOOM.

Ratburger

"Who have you got in there, you little squirt?" came a guttural voice from outside.

No! thought Zoe. *It's Tina Trotts.* The spit from today's flob had still not entirely come off Zoe's little freckled face.

Tina was only fourteen but built like a trucker. She had big hands that could punch, big feet that could kick, a big head that could butt, and a big butt that could squash.

Even the teachers were scared of her. Inside the cubicle, Zoe was quaking with fear.

"There's no one in here," said Zoe.

Why did I say that? she instantly thought. The mere act of saying that there was no one in there meant there was definitely, without doubt, one hundred per cent, someone in there.

Zoe was in terrible danger, but only if she opened the door. For now, she was safe inside the—

"Get out of the bog right now before I smash the door in!" threatened Tina.

Oh dear.

9

One Shoe

Zoe quickly put Armitage back in her blazer pocket.

"I am just having a wee!" said Zoe. Then she made a rather pitiful sound that she hoped would sound like water gushing into a bowl by pursing her lips and blowing. It ended up sounding more like a snake hissing.

"Pppppppppppppppppsssssssssssssssssss ssssssssssssssssSsssssssssssssssssSsssssssss.............."

Of course, Zoe's hope was that this would convince Tina Trotts that she was using the toilet for legitimate purposes only, and not for feeding a bread sandwich to a long-tailed rodent.

Zoe then took a deep breath and opened the toilet door. Tina stared down at Zoe, two of her usual goons flanking her.

"Hello, Tina," said Zoe in a voice quite a few octaves higher than her usual one. In attempting to play the innocent, she felt like she was giving the appearance of someone who was in fact exceedingly guilty.

"Oh, it's you! Who were you talking to, Braceface?" demanded Tina, leaning into the cubicle now.

"Myself," said Zoe. "I often actually talk to myself whenever I am passing water…"

"Passing wot?!"

"Um… having a wee? So if you will excuse me I have to be off to my History class…" With that, the little ginger girl tried to ease past Tina and her foot soldiers.

"Not so fast," said Tina. "Me and my gang own these bogs. We sell stolen gear from in 'ere. So unless you want to buy a trainer we nicked, sod off!"

"Don't you mean a pair of trainers?" enquired Zoe.

"No. I mean a trainer. They only put one out on the shelves so it's much easier to steal one than two."

"Mmmm," mused Zoe, not sure why anyone with two feet would want to buy just the one shoe.

"Listen, Ginge," continued the bully. "We don't want you in our bogs. You hear? Puttin' off all the customers by talking to yerself like some nutter…"

"Understood," muttered Zoe. "Very sorry, Tina."

"Now give us yer money," demanded Tina.

"I don't have any," replied Zoe. She wasn't lying. Her dad had been on benefits for years so she never ever received pocket money. When she walked to school she would scour the pavements for coins. One particularly lucky day she had found a five-pound note in a gutter! It was wet, it was dirty, but it was hers. Skipping home in delight, she stopped off at Raj's Newsagent and bought a whole box of chocolates to share with her family. However, before Zoe's dad had got home, her stepmother had scoffed every single one, even the dreaded cherry liqueurs, before gobbling down the box too.

"No money? Likely story," splattered Tina. Splattering is a bit like spluttering but the person being talked to ends up covered in spit.

"What do you mean?" said Zoe. "We both

live on the same estate. You know I don't have any cash."

Tina scoffed. "I bet you get pocket money. Always walking around like you own the place. Girls – grab her."

Like clockwork, the bullies circled our little heroine. The two goons seized her arms tightly.

"Aaah!" screamed Zoe in pain. Their fingernails were digging into her little arms as Tina's large dirty hands started rooting in Zoe's pockets.

Zoe's heart started pounding. Armitage the rat was lying asleep in the breast pocket of her blazer. Tina's chubby fingers were prodding and poking everywhere. Within seconds they would come into contact with a small rodent, and Zoe's life at school would change for ever.

Bringing a rat into school was not something you would ever live down.

Once, a boy a few years above had mooned out of the coach window on a school trip to the railway museum and ever since then he had only ever been called 'Hairy Bum' by everyone in the school, even the teachers.

Time slowed down and then speeded up as Tina's search for money led inevitably to Zoe's breast pocket. Her fingers thrust in and poked poor little Armitage on the nose.

"What's this?" said Tina. "The little ginge has got something living in there."

Now, Armitage must have not taken kindly to being prodded by a big dirty finger on the nose, because he bit into it.

"Aaaaaaaaaaaaaaaaaaaaaar rrrrrrrrrrrrrrrggggggggg gggggggggggggggghh hhhhhhhhhhh!!!!!!!!!!! !!!!!!!!!!!!!!!!!!!!!!!" screamed Tina.

Her hand shot out of Zoe's pocket, but Armitage was still attached, clinging on with his little sharp teeth, dangling from her finger.

"EEEEEEEEEEEEUUU UUUUUUUURRRRRRRR RRRGGGGGGGGGGGG HHHHHHHHHH!!!!!!!!!!!!!!! !!!!!!!!!!!!!!!!!!!!!" squealed the bully. "It's a rat!"

10

The Midget

"It's only a baby rat," reasoned Zoe, trying to calm Tina down. She was afraid she might smack Armitage against something and hurt him.

Tina started shaking her hand violently as she ran around the girls' toilets in utter panic. However, the baby rat would not let go. The goons stood as still as statues, searching their tiny brains for the appropriate response to 'rat attached to finger'.

Unsurprisingly, nothing seemed to come to mind.

"Hold still," said Zoe.

Tina kept running around.

"I said *hold still*."

Seemingly shocked by this authoritative tone from the small ginger girl, Tina stopped moving.

Carefully, as if dealing with an angry bear, Zoe took Tina's hand in hers. "Come on, Armitage…"

Carefully she prised the rat's sharp front teeth off the large girl's finger.

"There you go," said Zoe in the manner of a dentist who had just given a child a mildly painful filling. "Come on now. Tut-tut. It wasn't too bad."

"The little @**$$$$&!%^!%!!!! bit me!" protested Tina, revealing herself as the likely author of the insulting message on the toilet door. The bully examined her finger, two tiny drops of blood oozing out of the tip.

"Tina, they are nothing more than pin pricks," replied Zoe.

The two goons craned their long necks to get a closer look, and nodded their heads in agreement with Zoe. This infuriated Tina and her face went fiery red like a volcano about to explode.

There was an eerie silence for a moment.

I am about to die, thought Zoe. *She is actually going to kill me.*

Then the bell rang for the end of break.

"Well, if you'll excuse us," said Zoe, more calmly than she felt, "Armitage and I don't want to be late for our History class."

"Why is 'e called dat?" grunted one goon.

"Erm, it's a long story," said Zoe, who wasn't about to tell them he was named after a toilet. "Another time perhaps. Goodbye!"

The three bullies were too shocked to stop

her. Cupping her little friend in her hand, she strolled out of the toilets. Just clear of the door, she realised she wasn't actually breathing, and that she should probably start again. Then she gave Armitage a little kiss on the head.

"You are my guardian angel!" she whispered before placing him carefully back in her breast pocket.

Zoe suddenly realised Tina and her gang might be following her, so without looking back, she quickened her pace. The stroll became a stride and the stride became a sprint and before she knew it she was sitting breathless in her History class, which was presided over by Miss Midge. As the History teacher was an exceptionally short lady, she had inevitably been given the nickname 'Miss Midget', or more simply 'Midget'.

The teacher always wore knee-high leather boots with heels that made her look even shorter than she actually was. However, what Miss Midge lacked in height she made up

for in ferocity. Her teeth would not have been out of place in the mouth of a crocodile. She bared these teeth whenever a pupil displeased her, which was often. Kids didn't have to do much to infuriate her, even an

involuntary sneeze or a cough could result in a monstrous snarl from the terrifying but tiny teacher.

"You are late," growled Miss Midge.

"Sorry, Miss Midget," said Zoe, without thinking.

Oh no.

There were a few chuckles from her classmates, but mainly gasps. Zoe was so used to calling the History teacher 'Miss Midget' behind her back that she had done it to her face by mistake!

"What did you say?" demanded Miss Midge.

"I said 'sorry, Miss Midge'," spluttered Zoe. The sweat that had sprung up on her run from the girls' toilets was now teeming out of her pores. Zoe looked like she had been caught in a vicious thunderstorm. Armitage was squirming too, probably because the blazer pocket that had become his home was suddenly damp with warm sweat. It must be like a sauna in there! Surreptitiously, Zoe reached a hand up to her breast and patted gently to calm her little friend.

"One more piece of misconduct from you," said Miss Midge, "and you will not just be out of this classroom, you will be out of the school."

Zoe gulped. She had only just started at big school, and she wasn't used to getting into trouble. She had never done anything wrong at her little school, and even the *thought* of doing something wrong frightened her.

"Now, back to the lesson. Today you are going to learn more about... the Black Death!" pronounced Miss Midge, as she scrawled the words as high as she could reach on the board, which was actually the bottom.

Writing on the board was a real problem for Miss Midge, in fact. Sometimes she would order a child to get down on the classroom floor on their hands and knees.

The miniature teacher would then climb on top of them, so she could reach high enough to wipe the board clean of the previous teacher's scribbling. For very high scribblings from very tall teachers you simply stacked up more children.

The Black Death was not on the school history syllabus, but Miss Midge taught it anyway. Legend had it that one year all of her class failed their exam because instead of teaching them about Queen Victoria she spent a whole year relishing the gruesome details of the medieval torture of being hanged, drawn and quartered. Miss Midge would refuse to teach anything but the most grisly passages of history: beheadings, flogging, burning at the stake. The teacher would grin and bare her crocodile teeth at the mention of anything cruel and brutal and barbaric.

In fact, this term Miss Midge had been going on non-stop about the Black Death. It was her absolute obsession. Unsurprising really, as this was one of the darkest periods in human history, when in the fourteenth century 100 million people died from a terrifying infectious disease.

Victims would be covered in giant boils, vomit blood, and die. The cause, they had learned in the previous lesson, was nothing more than a fleabite.

"Boils the size of apples! Imagine that. Vomiting until all that was left to sick up was your own blood! They couldn't dig the graves fast enough! Wonderful stuff!"

The children stared at Miss Midge, open-mouthed with terror. At that moment the headmaster Mr Grave entered the classroom without knocking, his long coat flapping behind him like a cape. The naughty kids at the back of the class who had been texting throughout the lesson quickly hid their mobile phones under the desk.

"Ah, Mr Grave, to what do I owe the pleasure?" said Miss Midge, smiling. "Is it about the talent show?"

Zoe had long since suspected that Miss Midge had a soft spot for the headmaster. Only that morning, Zoe had passed a poster in the corridor for the end-of-term talent show that Miss Midge was putting on. The poster was of course placed very low down on the wall, really at knee height for most pupils. It seemed very out of character for Miss Midge to organise something so fun, and Zoe wondered if she had only done it to impress the headmaster. It was well known that Mr Grave, despite his scary vampire appearance, was a great lover of school plays and the like.

"Good morning, Miss Midget, I mean Miss Midge…" Even Mr Grave couldn't stop himself!

The History teacher's smile dropped.

"I am afraid it isn't about the talent show, though I am grateful to you for putting it on."

Miss Midge beamed again.

"No," boomed Mr Grave. "It's something

much more serious I'm afraid."

Miss Midge's smile dropped once more.

"You see," said the headmaster, "the caretaker has found a... a... dropping in the girls' toilets."

11

The Black Death

All the kids in the class started sniggering when the headmaster used the word 'dropping', except Zoe.

"Someone did a poo on the toilet floor, sir?!" asked one of the boys, laughing.

"Not a human dropping! An animal one!" shouted the headmaster. "Mr Bunsen, the head of Science, is studying it now to find out what animal it is from. But we suspect it to be some kind of rodent..."

Armitage wriggled, and Zoe gulped. A rogue dropping must have plopped out unnoticed on to the toilet floor.

Stay very, very still, Armitage, thought Zoe.

Unfortunately, Armitage was not a mind-reader.

"If any pupil considers it acceptable to bring a pet into this school, let me tell you it is forbidden. Strictly forbidden!" pronounced the headmaster from the front of the class.

It was funny seeing the two teachers stand next to each other for a moment, such was the height difference.

"Any pupil found smuggling an animal of any kind into school will be instantly suspended. That is all!" With that, he turned and left the room.

"Masterful! Goodbye, Mr Grave…!" called Miss Midge after him. She watched him go, wistfully. Then she turned back to her pupils. "Right, you heard Colin, I mean Mr Grave. It is forbidden to bring pets into school."

The kids all looked around at each other and started whispering.

"Bring a pet into school?" Zoe could hear them saying to each other. "Who would be so stupid?"

Zoe sat as still as she could, staring forward in silence.

"SILENCE!" snarled Miss Midge, and there was silence. "It is not an opportunity to talk! Now let's get back to the lesson. The Black Death." She underlined those three words on the board.

"So, how did the incredibly deadly disease travel all the way from China to Europe? Anybody?" asked the teacher without turning around. She was one of those teachers who asked questions but didn't wait for answers. So, a millisecond after posing the question, she herself answered it.

"Nobody? *Rats* brought the fatal disease. Rats, on board merchant ships."

Zoe couldn't feel Armitage squirming around any more, and breathed a sigh of relief. He must have gone to sleep.

"But it wasn't the rats' fault, was it?" blurted out Zoe, without putting her hand up. She couldn't believe her little friend's great great great great great great great grandparents could be responsible for such incredible suffering. Armitage was far too sweet to hurt a soul.

Miss Midge spun round on her heels (which despite being high still didn't make her even of medium height). "Did you speak, child?" she whispered, as if she was a witch incanting a spell.

"Yes, yes..." spluttered Zoe, now beginning to wish she had kept her mouth shut after all. "Forgive me, but I just wanted to say, Miss

Midge, that you shouldn't really blame the rats for this terrible disease, as it wasn't their fault. It was the fleas catching a free ride on their backs that are really to blame..."

All the kids in the class were now looking at Zoe in disbelief. Despite this being a rough school, and teachers often having to leave with nervous breakdowns, no one *ever* interrupted Miss Midge, especially not to spring to the defence of rats.

The classroom fell deathly silent. Zoe looked around. Every pair of eyes in the room was now glaring at her. Most of the girls looked disgusted, and most of the boys were laughing.

Then, suddenly, Zoe felt like she had a tremendous itchy itch on her head. Quite the itchiest itchy itch that had ever itched. It was, in a word, itchtastic.

What on earth is that...? she wondered.

"Zoe?" sneered Miss Midge, now staring intently at exactly the place where Zoe had the itch on her head.

"Yes, Miss?" asked Zoe, perfectly innocently.

"You have a rat on your head…"

12

Instant Suspension

What is the worst thing that could ever happen to you at school?

When you arrive in the morning, you walk through the playground and realise you forgot to put on any clothes except your school tie?

In an exam you become so nervous about getting the answers right and your stomach churns up so badly that your bum explodes?

During a football match you run around kissing all your team-mates after you have scored a goal, only to be told by the PE teacher that it was, in fact, an own goal?

You trace your family tree in a History class and you find out you are related to your headmaster?

You have a sneezing fit in front of the head teacher and cover them head to toe in snot?

It's fancy dress day at school but you get the date wrong and you spend the entire day dressed up as Lady Gaga?

You are playing Hamlet in William Shakespeare's play at school and halfway through the 'To be or not to be…' speech your Auntie rushes up from the audience, spits on a tissue and wipes your face with it?

You take off your trainers after games and the smell of mouldy cheese is so bad the entire school has to be closed down for a week to be de-fumigated?

At lunchtime in the dining hall you overdose on baked beans and you do a blow-off that lasts all afternoon?

You smuggle a rat into school in your blazer and it climbs up and sits on your head during a lesson?

Any of those would be enough to get you added to the list of infamous pupils – those famous for all the wrong reasons. With the 'rat on head' incident, Zoe was about to be on the list of shame for ever.

"You have a rat on your head," repeated Miss Midge.

"Oh, do I, Miss?" said Zoe, mock-innocently.

"Don't worry," said Miss Midge. "Sit very still, and we'll call for the caretaker. I'm sure he can kill it."

"Kill it! No!" Zoe reached on to her head and lifted the rodent over her now-even-more-wiry mess of red hair and held it in front of her. Children around her got up from their seats and backed away from her.

"Zoe... do you *know* this rat?" said Miss Midge, suspiciously.

"Um... no," said Zoe.

At this point, Armitage ran up her arm and climbed into her breast pocket.

Zoe looked down at him. "Er..."

"Did that rat just climb into your pocket?"

"No," said Zoe, ridiculously.

"It is clear," said Miss Midge, "that this filthy beast is your pet."

"Armitage is not a filthy beast!"

"Armitage?" said Miss Midge. "Why on earth is he called that?!"

"Oh, it's a long story, Miss. Look, he's safely in my pocket now. Please continue."

The teacher and the rest of the class were so gobsmacked by her casual response, for a moment no one knew what to say or do. The silence was deafening, but it didn't last.

"You heard what the headmaster said," roared Miss Midge. "Instant suspension!"

"But but but I can explain…"

"GET OUT! GET OUT OF MY CLASSROOM YOU VILE LITTLE GIRL! AND TAKE THAT DISGUSTING CREATURE WITH YOU!" snarled the teacher.

Without making eye contact with anyone, Zoe quietly gathered her books and pens and put them in her plastic bag. She pushed her chair back and it squealed against the shiny floor.

"Excuse me," said Zoe to no one in particular. As quietly as she could, she made her way to the door. She put her hand on the handle—

"I SAID 'INSTANT SUSPENSION'!"

yelled Miss Midge. "I DON'T WANT TO SEE YOU UNTIL THE END OF TERM!"

"Um… Bub-bye then," said Zoe, not sure of what else to say.

She opened the classroom door slowly, and closed it quietly behind her. Behind the frosted glass in the corridor she could see thirty distorted little faces press themselves up against it to watch her go.

There was a pause.

Then there was an enormous eruption of laughter, as the little girl made her way along the hall. Miss Midge yelled at them,

"SILENCE!"

With everyone still in class, the school felt strangely tranquil. All Zoe could hear were her own little footsteps echoing along the corridor, and the flapping of the rogue sole of her shoe. For a moment the drama of what had only just taken place seemed extremely distant, as if it had all happened in someone else's lifetime. School had never felt so eerily empty before, it was like this was a dream.

Yet if this was the calm after the storm, it wasn't to last long. The bell rang for lunch break, and like a dam bursting the classroom doors in the long corridor flung open and a blast of schoolchildren spurted out. Zoe quickened her pace. She knew the news of her having a rat on her head in History class would spread like the plague itself. Zoe had to get out of school, and fast…

13

Burt's Burgers

Soon Zoe noticed she was running, but her short little legs were no match for the older, taller kids, who were soon barging past her so they could be first in the queue at the burger van to stuff their faces at lunch.

Zoe shielded Armitage with her hand. She had been knocked to the ground in the school corridor so many times before. At last she made it out into the relative safety of the playground. She kept her head down, hoping not to be recognised.

However, there was only one way out of

the playground on to the main road. Every day there was the same grimy beaten-up burger van parked outside, which had 'Burt's Burgers' emblazoned across it. Even though the food from the van was horrible, the school dinners were even more nauseating, so most of the kids took the least worst option and queued up outside the van for their lunch.

Burt was as unsavoury as the burgers he served. The self-styled 'chef' always wore the same filthy striped top and grease-encrusted jeans, which he wore low below his giant belly. Over the top hung a bloody overall. The man's hands were always filthy, and his thick mop of hair was covered in flakes of dandruff the size of Rice Krispies. Even his dandruff had dandruff. The flakes would drop into the deep-fat fryer causing it to hiss and spurt whenever he leaned over it. Burt would

sniff constantly, like a pig snuffling in mud. No one had ever seen his eyes, as he always wore the same pitch-black, wraparound sunglasses. His false teeth rattled in his mouth whenever he spoke, causing him to whistle involuntarily. School legend had it that they had once fallen out of his mouth into a bap.

Burt's burger van didn't offer much of a menu:

BURGER IN A BAP 79P
BURGER ONLY 49P
BAP ONLY 39P

And there were no restaurant stars awarded as yet. The food was just about edible if you were absolutely starving. You had to pay an extra 5p for a squirt of ketchup, though it didn't look or taste much like ketchup; it was brown and had little black bits in it. If you complained, Burt would shrug and mutter breathlessly, "It's my own special recipe, my dears."

To Zoe's horror, Tina Trotts was already there, right at the front of the queue. If she hadn't been bunking off her lesson anyway, she would surely have intimidated her way to the front.

Spotting her, Zoe put her head down even

further, so that all she could see was the tarmac. But her head wasn't far enough down to go unrecognised.

"RAT-GIRL!" shouted Tina. Zoe popped her head up to see the long line of kids all looking at her. Some of her classmates were now in the queue as well, and all started pointing and laughing.

Soon it seemed like the whole of the school was laughing at her.

"HA HA HA HA HA HA HA HA HA HA HA HA HA HA HA HA HA HA HA HA HA HA HA HA HA HA HA HA HA HA HA HA HA HA HA HA HA HA !!!!!!!!! !!! !!! !!! !!!!!!!!!!!!!!!!!!!!!!!!!!"

Never had laughter sounded so cold. Zoe looked up for a moment. Hundreds of little eyes stared at her, but it was the figure of Burt, hunched over in his van, whose face she was drawn to. His nose was twitching, and a large gloop of slobbering saliva fell from the corner of his mouth into Tina's bap...

Zoe couldn't go home.

Her stepmother would be at the flat watching daytime TV, smoking fags and stuffing her face with prawn cocktail crisps. If Zoe told her why she had been suspended, there was no way she would be able to keep Armitage. Most likely Sheila would instantly exterminate him. With her big heavy foot. Zoe would have to peel him off the sole of her stepmother's furry pink slipper.

Quickly, Zoe considered her options:

1) Go on the run with Armitage and hold up banks like Bonnie & Clyde and go out in a blaze of glory.

2) Both have plastic surgery and then go and live in South America where no one would know them.

3) Tell her dad and stepmother that it was 'Adopt-a-Rodent' week at school and there was absolutely nothing to worry about.

4) Claim that Armitage was not a real rat but an animatronics one that she had made in Science class.

5) Say that she was training the rodent for some top-secret spy work for the Intelligence Service.

6) Give Armitage a white hat and paint him blue and pretend he was a toy Smurf.

7) Make two hot air balloons out of her stepmother's gigantic bra, one large and one small, and fly off the roof to another county.

8) Hijack a mobility scooter and speed off to safety.

9) Invent and build a dematerialisation machine and beam herself and Armitage to safety[5].

10) Just go to Raj's shop and have some sweets...

Unsurprisingly, Zoe chose the last option.

"Aah, Miss Zoe!" proclaimed Raj, as she opened the door to his shop. The bell rang as she entered.

TING.

"Shouldn't you still be in school, Miss Zoe?"

---

[5] *This may have been a teeny bit too complicated to achieve.*

Raj asked.

"Yes, I should," muttered Zoe, downcast. She felt as if she was about to burst into tears.

Raj rushed out from behind his counter and gave the little ginger girl a hug.

"What's the matter, young lady?" he asked, pressing her head to his big comfy belly. It was so long since anyone had given Zoe a hug. Unfortunately though, her braces got caught on his woollen cardigan, and for a moment she was stuck to him.

"Oh dear," said Raj. "Let me just detangle myself." He gently prised his cardigan from out of the metal.

"Sorry, Raj."

"No problem, Miss Zoe. Now, tell me," he began again, "what on earth has happened?"

Zoe took a deep breath and then told him. "I have been suspended."

"No?! You are such a well-behaved child. I don't believe it!"

"It's true."

"Whatever for?"

Zoe thought it might be easier to show him, so she reached into her breast pocket, and pulled out her rat.

"Aaaaaaaaaaaarrrrrrrrrrrr
rrggggggggggggggg

gggghhhhhhhhhhh
hhhhhhhh!!" screamed Raj.

He scuttled away and clambered up on top of the counter. There he stood for quite a while screaming.

"Aaaaaaaarrrrrrrrrrr
rggggggggggggggg
gggghhhh!!

"Aaaaaaaaarrrrrrrrrr
rrgggggggggghhh!!

"I don't like mice, Miss Zoe. Please please please, Miss Zoe. Please. I beg you. Put it away."

"Don't worry, Raj, it's not a mouse."

"No?"

"No, it's a rat."

Then Raj's eyes bulged and he let out a deafening scream.

"AAAAAAAAAA
AAAAAAAAAAAAAAAAAAAA
AAAAAAAAAAAAA
AAAAAAAAAAAAAAAAAAAAA
AAAAAAAAAAAAA
AAAAAAAAAAAAAARRR
RRRRRRRRRRRRRR
RRRRRRRRRRRRRR
RRRRRRRRRRRRRR
RRRRRRRRRRRRRrrr
RRRRRRRRRRRRRRRRR
RRRRRRRRRRRRRRRRR
RRRRRRRRRRRRRRRRRrr
RRRRRRRRRRRRRRRRR
RRRRRRRRRRRRRRRRRR
RRGGGGGGGGGGGGGGGGGGG
GGGGGGGGGGG
GGGGGGGGGGGGGGG
GGGGGGGGGGGGGGGGGGGG

GGGGGGGGGGGG
GGGGGGGGGGGGGGG
GGGGGGGGGGGGGGGGGGG
GGGGGGGGGGGG
GGGGGGGGGGGGGGGGGG
HHHHHHHHHHHH
HHHHHHHHHHHHHH
HHHHHHHHHHHH
HHHHHHHHHHHHHH
HHHHHHHHHHHH
HHHHHHHHHHHHHH
HHHHHHHHHHHH
HHHHHHHHHHHH!!!!!!!!!!!!!!!!!!!!!!!!!
!!!
!!!!!!!!!!!!!!!!!!!!!!!!!!!!!!!!!!!!
!!!!!!!!!!!!!!!!!!!!!!!!!!!!!!!!!!!!!!
!!!!!!!!!!!!!!!!!!!!!!!!!!!!!!!!!!!"

14

A Bogie on the Ceiling

"No, no, please," pleaded the newsagent. "I don't like it! I don't like it!"

TING!

An old lady entered the shop, and looked up bemused at the newsagent perched on top of his counter. Raj was clutching his trouser legs, what little hair he had on his head standing on end, and he was trampling all the newspapers in terror with his big clumsy feet.

"Ah, hello, Mrs Bennett," said Raj, his voice shaking. "Your *Knitting Weekly* is on the shelf, you can pay me next time."

"What on earth are you doing up there?" enquired the old lady, quite reasonably.

Raj looked over at Zoe. Surreptitiously, she put her finger to her mouth, imploring him not to tell. She didn't want everyone to know she had a rat, or soon the news would spread to the estate and her dreaded stepmother. Unfortunately, though, Raj was not a natural liar.

"Erm, um, well…"

"I just bought some Spacedust," said Zoe, stepping in. "You know, the popping sweets? It had been left out in the sun and became highly explosive and when I opened the bag it sprayed all over the shop."

"Yes, yes, Miss Zoe," chimed in Raj. "A most regrettable incident because it's only been fifteen years since I had the shop repainted. I am just trying to pick the Spacedust off the ceiling."

Raj came across a particularly ingrained piece of dirt on the ceiling and scratched at it. "Spacedust everywhere, Mrs Bennett. Please pay me next week…"

The old lady shot him an unconvinced look and peered up at the ceiling. "That's not Spacedust, that's just a piece of snot."

"No, no, no, Mrs Bennett, that's where you are wrong. Look…"

Reluctantly Raj used his fingernail to prise away the bogie he had long since sneezed up there and popped it in his mouth.

"Pop!" he added unconvincingly. "Oh, I love Spacedust!"

Mrs Bennett looked at the newsagent as if he was quite mad. "It looked more like a big piece of snot to me," she muttered before leaving the shop.

TING.

Raj quickly spat out the ancient bogie.

"Look, the little thing is not going to hurt you," said Zoe. She gently took him out of her pocket. Cautiously Raj clambered down, and slowly approached his worst nightmare.

"He's only a baby," said Zoe encouragingly.

Soon Raj was at eye level with the rodent.

"Ooh, well, he is a particularly pretty one. Look at his dinky little nose," said Raj with a sweet smile. "What's his name?"

"Armitage," answered Zoe confidently.

"Why is he called that?" asked Raj.

Zoe was embarrassed she had named her pet after a make of toilet and simply said, "Oh, it's a long story. Give him a stroke."

"No!"

"He won't hurt you."

"If you are sure…"

"I promise."

"Come here, little Armitage," whispered the newsagent.

The rat squirmed closer to Raj to be stroked by this frightened-looking man.

"AAAAAAHHHHH! HE MADE A LUNGE AT ME!" shouted Raj, and with that he ran out of the shop waving his arms in the air…

TING.

Zoe followed him out, and saw he was halfway down the street, running so fast he would give the Olympic-gold-winning sprinters a run for their money.

"COME BACK!" she shouted.

Raj stopped and turned round, and reluctantly plodded back past the row of shops to his one. When he finally tiptoed the last few paces towards the girl and her pet, Zoe said, "He was just trying to say hello."

"No, no, no, sorry, but he got quite close."

"Don't be a baby, Raj."

"I know, sorry. He's lovely really."

Raj took a deep breath, and reached out to give Armitage the gentlest little stroke. "It's nippy out. Let's take him inside."

TING.

"What am I going to do with him, Raj? My stepmother won't let me keep him at home, especially as the little fella got me suspended from school. That woman hated my hamster, she is never in a million years going to let me keep a rat."

Raj thought for a moment. To aid concentration he popped an extra strong mint in his mouth.

"Maybe you should set him free," said the newsagent finally.

"Free?" said Zoe, a single tear welling in her eye.

"Yes. Rats are not meant to be pets…"

"But this little one is so cute…"

"Perhaps, but he is going to grow. He can't spend his whole life in your blazer pocket."

"But I love him, Raj, I really do."

"No doubt, Miss Zoe," said Raj, crunching on his extra strong mint. "And if you love him, you should set him free."

15

Ten-Tonne Truck

So this was goodbye. Zoe knew deep down she would never be able to keep Armitage for long. There were a hundred reasons, but the most important one was:

HE WAS A RAT.

Children don't have rats as pets. They have cats and dogs and hamsters and gerbils and guinea pigs and mice and rabbits and terrapins and tortoises, posh ones even sometimes have ponies, but never rats. Rats live in sewers, not in little girls' bedrooms.

Zoe trudged miserably out of Raj's shop.

The newsagent may sometimes try and sell his customers a half-eaten chocolate bar, or put a partially sucked toffee bonbon back in the sweet jar, but all the local kids knew that when it came to advice he was the best.

And that meant she had to say goodbye to Armitage.

So Zoe took the long way back to her flats, through the park. She thought this would be the perfect place to set little Armitage free. There would be crusts of bread left out for the ducks for him to eat, a pond for him to drink from and maybe even take the occasional bath in, and perhaps there was a squirrel or two whom he could befriend, or at least one day be on nodding terms with.

The little girl carried the little rat in her hand for the last part of the journey. As it was the middle of the afternoon, the park was all but empty save for a few old ladies being walked by their dogs. Armitage wrapped his tail around her thumb. It was almost as if he sensed something was amiss, and he clung on to her little fingers as tightly as he could.

Trudging along as slowly as possible, Zoe eventually reached the middle of the park. She stopped a good distance from the yapping dogs and hissing swans and barking park-keeper. Slowly she crouched down to the ground and unclosed her hand. Armitage didn't move. It was as if he didn't want to be parted from his new friend. He cuddled up to her hand, breaking Zoe's heart as he did it.

Zoe shook her hand a little, but this only made him grip tighter with his tail and toes. Fighting back tears she picked the rat up gently by the fur on the back of his neck and placed him carefully on the grass. Once again Armitage didn't move.

Instead he just looked up at her longingly. Zoe knelt down and kissed him gently on his little pink nose.

"Goodbye, little fellow," she whispered. "I am going to miss you."

A tear dropped from her eye. It landed on Armitage's whiskers and his tiny pink tongue slipped out to catch it.

The little rat tilted his little head to one side, as if trying to understand her, which just made it harder for Zoe.

In fact, saying goodbye was so unbearably sad, she just couldn't take it any more. Zoe took a big breath and stood up, and promised herself she would not look back. That promise lasted only a dozen steps, as she couldn't help stealing a glance one last time to the spot where she left him. To Zoe's surprise, Armitage was already gone.

He must have already scampered off to the safety of the bushes, she thought. She scoured the nearby grass for signs of movement, but it was tall and he was short, and apart from a light breeze blowing the tips, the grass didn't move. Zoe turned round and reluctantly headed home.

Leaving the park, she crossed the road. For a moment it was free of the hum of cars, and in the silence, Zoe thought she heard a tiny 'eek'. She spun round, and in the middle of the road was Armitage.

He had been following her all along.

"Armitage!" she exclaimed excitedly. He didn't want to be free; he wanted to be with her! She was so glad. She had been imagining all kinds of awful scenarios from the moment she left him behind – like Armitage being gobbled up by a vicious swan, or wandering into the road and being hit by a ten-tonne truck.

At that moment something came thundering along the road towards Armitage, who was still scampering slowly across to join Zoe.

It was... a ten-tonne truck.

Zoe stood frozen, watching the truck speeding closer and closer towards Armitage. The driver would never spot a baby rat in the road, and Armitage would be flattened, and be nothing more than a splat on the tarmac...

"NNNNNNNNNOOO OOOOOOOOOOOOOOOO OO!!!!" cried Zoe, but the truck thundered on. There was nothing she could do.

Armitage looked in the direction of the truck and, realising he was in trouble, started scampering back and forth across the road. The little rat was in a terrible panic. But if Zoe ran into the road she would be flattened too!

It was too late. The truck roared over him

and Zoe covered her eyes with her hands.

RRRRrrrrrrrrrr
RRUUUUUUUUUUUUU
UUUUUUMMmmmmm
MMMMMMMMB
BBBBBBBBBBB
BBBBBBBBBLL
LLLLLLLLL
LLLLLLEEEE
EEEEEEEE!!!!!!
!!!!!!!!!!!!!!!!!!!!!!!

Only when she could hear the truck's engine fading into the distance did Zoe dare open her eyes again.

She looked for the splat on the road.

But it wasn't there.

What was there... was Armitage! A little

shaken perhaps, but alive. The lorry's giant tyres must have just missed him.

Looking right and left and right again to check there were no cars, Zoe ran into the road and scooped him up.

"I am not letting go of you, ever," said Zoe, as she held him close. Armitage let out a little loving 'eek'…

16

The Blackberry Bush

Nature finds a way to create life everywhere. In a smelly alleyway that connected the road to Zoe's estate, among all the crisp wrappers and empty beer cans, stood a proud little blackberry bush. Zoe loved the blackberries – they were like free sweets. She was pretty sure Armitage would like them too. She picked a large one for herself, and a little one for her furry friend.

Carefully, she placed the baby rat on to the wall. As Armitage watched, Zoe put the blackberry into her mouth and started chewing enthusiastically and making appreciative noises.

Then she took the smaller blackberry between her thumb and forefinger and held it out towards him. Armitage must have been hungry because slowly he stood up on his hind legs to greet it.

Zoe was delighted. The rat took the blackberry between his front paws and nibbled it greedily. It was gone in seconds. Soon he was looking longingly up at Zoe for another one. She picked another off the bush and held it up just above his nose. Without hesitation, Armitage stood up on his hind legs again. Zoe moved the blackberry around, and he followed it around on his back legs. It was as if he was doing a little dance.

"What a talented fellow you are!" said Zoe, as she gave him the blackberry. Once again he ate it greedily, and Zoe stroked the back of his neck. "Good boy!"

Inside, she was buzzing with excitement. Armitage could be trained! Better still, it was like he *wanted* to be. He'd got the idea of standing up even quicker than Gingernut had…

Soon Zoe was plucking as many blackberries as she could off the bush. Just as she had with her hamster, she began teaching Armitage some tricks. There was:

The walk.

The jump.

The hop on one leg.

The wave.

The dance.

Soon the bush was bare, and Armitage looked rather stuffed and tired. Zoe knew it was time to stop. She whisked him up in her arms and gave him a kiss on his nose.

"You are amazing, Armitage. That's what I will call you when we perform together on stage. The Amazing Armitage!"

Zoe skipped down the alleyway. Her heart was dancing, as were her feet.

It was only when Zoe reached her estate that the spring in her step vanished. Not only would she have to tell her stepmother that she was suspended, she'd have to come up with some explanation as to why.

The whole episode would give her stepmother a reason to make Zoe's life even more of a living hell. And what was a million times worse, a reason to end the little rat's life. A life that had only just begun.

As Zoe approached the great leaning tower block, she noticed something peculiar. Burt's burger van was parked right outside her towering block of flats. In the many years she had lived there since her mother died, she had never ever seen the van there before. It was only *ever* parked outside her school.

What on earth is that doing there? she thought.

Even from a distance, the smell of fried meat was stomach-churning. However hungry Zoe was, she had never bought a burger from Burt's van. The stench alone was enough to make her want to projectile-vomit. The ketchup was decidedly iffy too. Passing the van, she noticed how disgustingly grimy it was – even the dirt was dirty. Zoe ran her index finger along the chassis, and a splodge of sludge an inch thick came off in her hand.

Perhaps Burt has just moved into the block

of flats, she thought. She hoped not though, as he was seriously creepy. Burt was the sort of man your nightmares had nightmares about.

The tiny flat was high up on the 37th floor, but the lift always stank. You had to hold your breath in there, which wasn't easy over thirty-seven floors. So Zoe would always take the stairs. Armitage was safely lying in her blazer pocket, and she could feel the weight of his tiny body bounce against her heart with every step. Her breathing grew louder and louder as she ascended the building. The stairs were littered with all kinds of rubbish, from cigarette butts to empty bottles. The steps stank too, but not as much as the lift, and of course you weren't so closed in.

As usual, by the time Zoe reached the 37th floor, she was completely breathless and panting like a dog. Zoe stood outside the front door for a moment, pausing to catch her breath before she put her key in the lock. The headmaster Mr Grave would no doubt have called her parents to tell them their daughter had been suspended. Within seconds, Zoe was sure to let loose her stepmother's fury, a fury no doubt more rabid even than the hounds of hell.

Zoe silently twisted the key, and reluctantly pushed the rotting door open. Even though her stepmother rarely went out, the TV was off and Zoe couldn't hear anyone in the house, so she tiptoed across the hall to her bedroom, being careful to avoid the squeakiest floorboards. She turned the door handle to her room and stepped inside.

A strange man was standing in her bedroom facing the window.

"Aaaaaahhhhhh!!!!!!!" Zoe screamed, startled.

Then the man turned round.

It was Burt.

17

"I Smell a Rat!"

"I smell a rat!" wheezed Burt.

Except it wasn't Burt. Well, it *was* Burt, but he had drawn a moustache on his face very poorly with a marker pen.

"What on earth are *you* doing here?" said Zoe. "And why have you got a moustache drawn on your face?"

"It is a real moustache, my dear," said Burt. He breathed heavily when he spoke. His voice matched his face: they had both stepped out of a horror film.

"No, it's not. You've drawn it on."

"No, I haven't."

"Yes, you have, Burt."

"My name is not Burt, child. I am Burt's twin brother."

"What's your name then?"

Burt thought for a moment. "Burt."

"Your mum had twins and called them both 'Burt'?"

"We were very poor and we couldn't afford a name each."

"Just get out of my room, you creep!"

All of a sudden Zoe heard her stepmother pound along the corridor. "Don't ya dare speak to the nice pest control man like dat!" she screeched, as she waddled into the room.

"He's not the pest control man. He sells burgers!" protested Zoe.

Burt stood between them with a smirk on his face. It was impossible to see what his eyes were doing because his wraparound sunglasses were black as the deepest, darkest oil.

"Wot are ya talkin' about, ya stupid girl? He catches rats," shouted Zoe's stepmother. "Don't ya?"

Burt nodded silently and smiled, flashing his ill-fitting false teeth.

The little girl grabbed her stepmother by her thick tattooed forearm, and led her to the window.

"Look at his van!" she declared. "Tell me

what's written on the side!"

Sheila looked out of the grimy window, to the vehicles parked down below. "Burt's Pest Control," she read.

"What?" said Zoe.

She wiped some of the smudges off the window, and peered out. The woman was right. It did say that. How was it possible? It looked like the same van. Zoe looked over at Burt. His smirk had widened. As she watched, he took a dirty little brown paper bag out of his pocket, and picked something out of it. Zoe could have sworn whatever he put in his mouth was moving. Could it have been a cockroach? Was that this depraved man's idea of a snack?!

"See?" said Burt. "I'm a rat catcher."

"Whatever," said Zoe. She turned to her stepmother. "Even if he is, which he isn't because he's a burger-van man, why is he in my *bedroom*?" she demanded.

"He is 'ere coz he 'eard at school dat ya brought a rat into ya lessons," replied her stepmother.

"It's a lie!" said Zoe, lying.

"Den why did I get a call from your 'eadmaster today? Eh? EH? ANSWER ME! 'E told me everyfink. Ya disgusting little girl."

"I don't want any trouble, my dear," said Burt. "Just hand the little creature over." He held out his grubby and gnarled hand. Burt had a dirty old cage on the floor by his feet that looked like it was made from a metal basket from a deep-fat fryer. Only instead of using it to fry chips, he had squashed hundreds and hundreds of rats into it.

At first glance, Zoe thought the rats were dead, as they weren't moving. On closer inspection, she realised they were alive, it was just they were packed in so tight they could hardly move. Many looked like they could hardly breathe either, they were all so squashed in together. It was a sickening sight, and Zoe wanted to cry at the shocking cruelty of it.

Just then Zoe felt Armitage wriggling in her breast pocket. Perhaps he could smell fear. The little girl discreetly brought her hand up to her breast to hide the wriggles. Her mind was racing with potential lies, before she arrived at one.

"I set him free," she said. "The headmaster is right, I did bring a rat into school, but I set him free in the park. Just ask Raj – he told me to do it. You should go and look for the rat in the park," she added, suddenly cupping Armitage through her blazer pocket, as the little rodent was squirming like crazy now.

There was a deathly pause. Then Burt sneered, "You are lying, my dear."

"I'm not!" said Zoe, a little too quickly.

"Don't lie to the nice man," bellowed Sheila. "We can't 'ave another filthy disease-ridden creature runnin' around the flat."

"I'm not lying," protested Zoe.

"I can smell it," said the vile man, his vile nose twitching. "I can smell a rat from miles away."

Burt sniffed the air, then wheezed. "Baby ones smell especially sweet…" He licked his lips, and Zoe shuddered.

"There's no rat here," said Zoe.

"Hand it over," said Burt. "Then I give it a quick whack with this special high-tech rodent stunner." He produced a bloody mallet from his back pocket. "It's painless really, they don't feel a thing. Then he can join his friends for a nice play in here." Burt indicated the cage, by kicking it hard with the heel of his dirty boot.

Zoe was horrified, but composed herself before she spoke. "You are quite wrong, I am afraid. There is no rat here. If it comes back we will of course call you immediately. Thank you."

"Hand it over. Now," wheezed the sinister man.

Meanwhile, Sheila was studying the step-daughter she loathed intently, and noticed the awkward positioning of her left hand.

"Ya vile creature!" accused the woman, as she yanked her stepdaughter's hand away. "It's in her blazer."

"Madam, you hold her down," directed Burt. "I can whack the rat through the cloth. There will be less blood on the carpet that way."

"Nooooooooooooooooo!" screamed Zoe. She tried to wrestle her arm away from her stepmother, but the woman was a lot bigger and stronger than her stepdaughter. The little girl lost her balance and crashed to the floor. Armitage wriggled out of her pocket and started scurrying across the carpet.

"Aaaaaaaaaaaaaaaaaaaa aaahhhhhhhhhhhhhhhh hhhhhhhh!!!!!!!!!!!!!! !!!!" screamed her stepmother. "Get it away from me!"

"Trust me, he won't feel a thing," wheezed Burt, as he got down on his hands and knees, brandishing the bloody mallet. His nose twitched as he chased the rat around the room, whacking the implement on to the floor, missing Armitage by millimetres.

"Stop!" screamed Zoe. "You'll kill him!"

She tried to make a charge at the man, but her stepmother held her back by her arms.

"Come here, you little beauty!" whispered Burt, as he brought the mallet crashing down repeatedly on to the dusty carpet, plumes of ingrained dirt now exploding into the air with every thwack.

Armitage scurried this way and that, trying desperately to avoid being whacked. The mallet walloped down, just catching his tail.

"Eeeeeeekkkkkkkkk!"

squealed the rat in pain, and he dashed off to

hide under Zoe's bed. This did not deter Burt, who, without taking off his dark glasses, got down on to his belly and slithered under the bed like a snake, flailing his mallet wildly from side to side.

Zoe writhed out of her stepmother's grasp and launched herself on to the man's back as soon as he appeared from under the bed. The little girl had never hit anyone before, and now she had leaped astride his back like a cowboy on a bull at an American rodeo, thumping his shoulders with all her might.

Within seconds her stepmother yanked her off by her hair and pinned her against the wall, before Burt disappeared under the bed again.

"Zoe, no! You're an animal. Ya 'ear me? An animal!" screamed the woman. Zoe had never seen her stepmother so uncontrollably angry.

Muffled under the bed, Zoe could hear thud

after thud of the mallet crashing down on the carpet. Tears were streaming down the girl's face. She couldn't believe her beloved little friend was going to meet such a violent end.

THWaCK!

And then there was silence. Burt wriggled out from under the bed. Exhausted, he sat on the floor. In one hand he held the bloody mallet. Between the fingers of his other hand he held a lifeless Armitage, dangling by his tail, before announcing triumphantly…

"Gotcha!"

18

"Pulverisation"

"Prawn cocktail crisp?" offered Sheila to the man.

"Mmm, don't mind if I do," Burt replied.

"Just one."

"Sorry."

"So, er, wot 'appens to all these rats?" continued Sheila in her poshest voice as she showed Burt to the door. Zoe was sitting crying on her bed. Her stepmother was so appalled by Zoe's behaviour she had locked her in her room. As much as Zoe rattled the handle and banged on the door, it wouldn't move. The little girl was utterly broken. There was nothing to do but weep. She listened to her stepmother show the repulsive man out.

"Well I tell the kiddies…" replied Burt in a tone that was meant to be reassuring but actually sounded disturbing, "…that they all go to a special hotel for rats."

Sheila laughed. "And they believe ya?"

"Yes, the little fools think they all get to frolic outdoors in the sunshine, before relaxing in a spa area, having massages and facials and the like!"

"But really…?" whispered Sheila.

"I pulverise them! In my special pulverisation machine!"

Sheila let out a gurgling laugh. "Is it painful?"

"Very!"

"Ha ha! Good. Do ya stamp on 'em?"

"No."

"Oh, I would stamp on 'em and then pulverise them. Then they would suffer twice as much!"

"I must try that, Mrs…?"

"Oh, just call me Sheila. Another prawn cocktail crisp?"

"Ooh, yes please."

"Just one."

"Sorry. Such a delicate flavour," mused Burt.

"Exactly like a real prawn cocktail, I dunno how they do it."

"Have you ever had a real prawn cocktail?"

"Nah," replied the woman. "But I don't need to. They taste just the same as the crisps."

"But of course. Madam, if you don't mind me saying, you are an extremely beautiful woman. I would love to take you out for dinner tonight."

"Oh, ya naughty man!" flirted Zoe's stepmother.

"Then I can treat you to one of my very special burgers."

"Ooh, yeah please!" The horrific woman added another sickeningly girly little laugh at the end. Zoe couldn't believe her stepmother was actually flirting so outrageously with this loathsome individual.

"Just me, you and all the burgers we can stuff down our gobs…" mused Burt.

"How romantic…" whispered Sheila.

"Until later, my Princess…"

Zoe heard the door close, and her stepmother thunder back along the corridor to her daughter's bedroom, before unlocking the door.

"You're in so much trouble, young lady!" said Sheila. She must have kissed Burt goodbye because she now had black marker pen above her lip.

"I don't care!" said Zoe. "All I care about is Armitage. I have to save him."

"Who's Armitage?!"

"He's the rat."

"Why would ya call a rat that?" asked the woman, incredulous.

"It's a long story."

"Well it's a completely stupid name for a rat."

"What would you call him?"

Sheila thought for a long while.

"Well?" asked Zoe.

"I'm finkin'."

A long silence followed during which Sheila looked like she was concentrating very hard. Finally she said, "Ratty!"

"A bit unoriginal," muttered Zoe.

That made her stepmother even more furious.

"You're evil. Ya know that, young lady. Evil! I've got a good mind to throw ya out on to the street! How could ya attack dat lovely man?"

"Lovely?! The man is a rat murderer!"

"No, no, no. They all go to a special rat sanctuary and have spa treatments…"

"Do you think I am completely stupid? He kills them."

"He doesn't stamp on 'em though. They are just pulverised. Shame, really."

"That's monstrous!"

"Who cares? One less rat."

"No. I have to save my little Armitage. I have to—"

Zoe stood up and headed for the door. Her stepmother pressed her firmly back down on to the bed with her considerable weight.

"You're not goin' anywhere," said the woman. "Yer grounded. Ya hear me? G-R-O-N-D-E-D! Grounded!"

"There's a 'U' in grounded," said Zoe.

"No dere isn't!" Sheila was really angry now. "Ya aint leaving dis room until I say so. Ya can sit in 'ere, fink about what ya 'ave done. And rot!"

"Wait until my dad gets home!"

"What's dat useless git gonna do?"

Zoe's eyes stung. Dad might have fallen on hard times, but he was still her father. "Don't you dare talk about him like that!"

"All he's good for is benefit money and a roof over me 'ead."

"I'll tell him you said that."

"He knows it already. I tell 'im every night," snorted the gruesome lady, with a guttural laugh.

"He loves me. He won't let you treat me like this!" protested Zoe.

"If 'e loves ya so much, why does he spend his whole life down de boozer?"

Zoe fell silent. She didn't have an answer to that. The words broke her heart into millions of tiny pieces.

"Ha!" said the woman. With that Sheila slammed the door shut and locked it behind her.

Zoe rushed to the window and peered down at the road. She had a pretty good view of it, what with being thirty-seven floors up in the crumbling tower block. In the distance, she could see Burt speeding off in his van. He wasn't much of a driver: she watched as he knocked off a few car wing mirrors and nearly ran over an old lady, before the van zoomed off out of view.

Outside, the sky grew dark, but the thousands of streetlights in the town lit up the outside world. They bathed her room in an ugly orange glow that could never be turned off.

Late into the evening, Dad finally returned from the pub. There was shouting between him and Sheila as there always was, and the slamming of doors. Dad never came into Zoe's bedroom to see her; most likely he had fallen asleep on the sofa before he had the chance.

Night came and went without sleep for Zoe. Her head was spinning and her heart was aching. In the morning she heard her dad go out, presumably to wait for the pub to open, and her stepmother turn on the TV. Zoe banged and banged on the door, but her stepmother would not let her out.

I am a prisoner, thought Zoe. She lay back down on her bed in despair, thirsty, hungry and desperately needing a wee.

Now what do prisoners do? she said to herself. *They try to escape…!*

19

The Great Escape

Armitage was in terrible danger. Zoe needed to save him. And fast.

She remembered that Burt parked his filthy burger van outside her school every day, so if she could just break out of her room she could follow him. Then she could find where he imprisoned all the rats before they were 'pulverised'.

Zoe pondered all the different ways in which she might try to escape:

1. She could tie all her bed sheets together, then try and abseil to safety.

Though, as she lived on the 37th floor, she wasn't sure the sheets would get her much further down than the 24th. Chance of death – high.

2. There was always the birdman option. Make some kind of glider from coat-hangers and knickers and fly down to freedom. Chance of death – high; and more importantly Zoe didn't have enough pairs of clean knickers.

3. Dig. Tunnels had been a favourite method of escape for soldiers in prisoner of war camps. Chance of death – low.

The problem with number three was that below Zoe's room was the flat of a moany old lady who, despite having the yappiest dogs herself, always went on and on about the noise from above. She would turn Zoe in to her stepmother in no time.

I could always tunnel sideways! thought Zoe.

She unstuck a poster of the latest boy band, and gently tapped the wall behind it with her fingernails. The tapping echoed into the next flat, which meant the wall must be thin. Over the years she had heard a great deal of shouting coming from next door, but it was too muffled to deduce what kind of people lived there – a girl and her parents, Zoe thought, but maybe others too. Whoever they were though, their lives sounded every bit as miserable as Zoe's, if not more so.

The plan itself was simple. The poster could be replaced at any time to hide what was going on. All she needed now was something to tunnel through the wall with. Something metal and sharp. *A key*, she thought, and ran excitedly to the door, only to remember that the key was on the other side. That was the whole reason she had to escape!

Duh! she said to herself.

Zoe rummaged through her belongings, but her ruler, her comb, her pen and her hangers were all made of plastic. Anything plastic would snap instantly if she tried to hollow out a wall with it.

Zoe caught sight of herself in the mirror and realised the answer was staring her in the face. Her braces. The blasted things would at last be of some use[6]. Zoe pulled them out with her fingers, and dashed to the wall. Without even pausing to wipe the spit off them she scratched at the wall. No wonder the braces were painful and rubbed against her gums, and got stuck in Raj's cardigan – the metal was sharp! Quickly the plaster from the wall was flaking on to the

---

[6] *Other than straightening teeth, of course. (I have to write that, as otherwise any orthodontists reading might make a complaint, even though they are all nothing more than blood-thirsty torturers.)*

floor. Soon Zoe had scratched through the plaster to the bricks behind it, and the braces became thick with all the paint and plaster and dust from the wall.

Suddenly Zoe heard the key in the lock turn in her bedroom door and she leaped up and stuck the poster back on the wall. Just in time, she remembered to shove her braces back in her mouth, though there wasn't time to wipe them first.

Sheila looked at her stepdaughter suspiciously. She looked like she knew Zoe was up to something, but she didn't know what. Yet.

"Do ya want some grub? I suppose I betta feed ya," said the vile woman. "If ya starve to death I'll have social services all over me like a bleedin' rash." Sheila's beady little eyes circled the room. Something was definitely different. She just couldn't quite put her chubby finger on it.

Zoe shook her head. She didn't dare speak with her mouth full of dust. In truth she was starving, but she had to get on with her escape plan, and didn't want any more interruptions.

"Ya must need to use the bog?" said the big lady.

Zoe spotted her stepmother's gaze searching the room. The little girl shook her head again. She thought she was going to choke, the dust now seeping right down the back of her throat. In truth she was bursting and she kept on having to cross her legs, but if she went to the loo and her stepmother searched her room she might just find the beginnings of the tunnel.

"'Ave ya got ya braces in?"

Zoe nodded vigorously, and then attempted a closed-mouth smile.

"Show me," pressed her stepmother.

Zoe slowly opened her mouth a little bit, to show a little bit of metal.

"I can't see. Wider!"

Reluctantly the girl opened her mouth, displaying the braces caked in dust. The woman peered to have a closer look.

"Ya need to clean your teef, they're disgustin'. Nasty creature you are."

Zoe closed her mouth and nodded in agreement. Sheila looked at her stepdaughter one last time and shook her head in revulsion, before turning to leave.

Zoe smiled. She had got away with it. For now.

She waited to hear the key turn in the door, and then turned towards the wall. Her boy-band poster was upside down! She prayed the one with the back to front hair would never find out she had put the poster upside down – he was Zoe's favourite and they were going to get married. He just didn't know it yet.

And on a slightly more urgent note: thank goodness her stepmother had missed the fact that the poster was no longer the right way up. Zoe spat out her braces and wiped her dry-as-a-desert tongue on her sleeve to try and remove the dust, then went back to work.

All through the night she scratched and scratched through the wall until finally she broke through. Her braces were now a misshapen mess, and she tossed them aside. So happy to be nearly there, Zoe excitedly let her fingers take over now. Scratching away to make the hole bigger, crumbling bits of plaster off in her hands as fast as she possibly could.

Zoe wiped her eyes and peered through the hole. She had no idea what would be on the other side. Taking a closer look she realised she could see a face.

A face she knew.

It was Tina Trotts.

20

Tug of War

Of course, Zoe had always known that the bully lived somewhere in her block of flats. Her gang permanently occupied the adventure playground. What's more, every day Tina spat on Zoe's head from a stairwell, but Zoe had no idea the horrible girl lived this close!

Then Zoe had a thought that made her feel confused: this meant it was Tina's family who shouted at each other and slammed doors more than even her own. It was Tina who got screamed at by her dad. And whom Zoe had felt sorry for, as she lay trying to get to sleep at night.

Zoe shook her head, to get rid of this strange new sensation of feeling *sorry* for Tina Trotts. Then she reminded herself of another sensation – flob on her face – and she stopped.

It was now mid-morning. Zoe had been scratching away at the wall all through the night. On the other side of the hole was Tina's big ugly face, snoring. She was lying on her bed, which, as if in a mirror image, was placed in exactly the same place as Zoe's was in her room. The room was bare of possessions though; it looked more like a prison cell than a girl's bedroom.

Tina was wrapped up in her grubby duvet. For a young girl she snored like a camel, loud and low, and her lips wobbled when she exhaled.

If you have ever wondered what a snoring camel sounds like, it goes something like this:

ZZZZZZZZZZZZZZ zzzzZZZZzzzzZzzzzzzzzzzz!

HHHHHHMM
MMMMMMMPPPP
PPPPPPPPPHHH
HHHHHHHHHHH!
ZZZZZZZZZZZZZ
ZZZZZZZzzzZZZ
zzzzZZZZzzzZZZ
ZZZzzzzzz!

It was a school day and Tina should be in lessons by now, but Zoe knew that most days she bunked off and when she didn't, she came and went as she pleased.

Now Zoe was face to face with her worst enemy. Yet there was no turning back. Everything in Zoe's room was covered in a thick dust as a result of her excavations. As soon as her stepmother unlocked the door to come in to check up on her, it would be game over, and she would never ever see Armitage again...

Right now, though, Tina's big scary face was right on the other side of the hole. Zoe peered at the bully's surprisingly thick nostril hair wondering what on earth to do next.

Suddenly Zoe thought of a plan. If only she could grab a corner of Tina's duvet, she could tug it sharply through the hole. Then, as Tina rolled on to the floor, Zoe could climb through the hole, jump over her, and bolt out through Tina's flat to safety.

It now occurred to her that she should revise the chance of death for the digging plan to 'high'.

At that moment, she heard her stepmother's footsteps thundering down the corridor.

Zoe had to act, and fast. She reached her hand through the hole, took a deep breath, and tugged as hard as she could on the duvet, which was rather greasy to the touch. It was as if it had never been washed. The yank was hard enough to send Tina rolling on to the floor…

THUD
THUD
THUD!

Just as Zoe heard the key turning in her bedroom door, she clambered through the hole. Unlike a rat, though, Zoe didn't have whiskers, and even though she was an unusually small girl she had rather underestimated her size. When her body was halfway through the hole, she became completely and utterly stuck. Try as she might to wriggle, she could not move an inch. Tina had now of course woken up, and it would be an understatement to say she did not look in a good mood. She was angrier than a great white shark that had been called a rude name.

The bully rose slowly to her feet, looked at

Zoe and started pulling violently at the small girl's arms, doubtless so she could get her whole body through to her room and beat her up more thoroughly.

"I am going to get you, you little runt," she growled.

"Oh, good morning, Tina," said Zoe, her tone imploring a non-violent response to this unusual situation. Meanwhile, no doubt hearing all the commotion, Sheila had rushed into the bedroom behind her and grabbed hold of her stepdaughter's legs. The odious woman was pulling as hard as she could on them.

"Come 'ere! When I get me 'ands on ya!" screamed the big lady.

"Good morning, stepmother," called Zoe over her shoulder. Again the chirpy tone did nothing to pacify the woman holding on to her ankles.

Soon Zoe was buffeting back and forward through the hole.

"Oooh!" she cried as she was pulled one way.

"Aaah!" she cried as she was pulled the other.

Soon it was like she was singing a rather repetitive pop song.

"Oooh! Aaah! Oooh! Aaah! Oooh! Aaaah! Oooh! Aaah! Oooh! Aaaah! Oooh! Aaah!"

Backward. Forward. Backward. Forward.

Soon after that the wall started crumbling around her as she was yanked back and forth.

Tina was strong, but Zoe's stepmother had weight on her side. It was a surprisingly even tug of war, which as a result felt like it would never end. Both were pulling so hard on Zoe's limbs that as she screamed she was aware of one positive to the situation: whoever won, Zoe would at least be taller by the end of it.

She felt like a particularly prized Christmas cracker. However, just like a Christmas cracker, she was sure to explode. Larger bits of plaster

were now crumbling off the wall, and dropping
on to her head.

"AAAAAAAAAAAAAAAAAAAAAARRRRRRRRRRGGGGGGGGHHHHHHH!!!!"

cried Zoe.

A massive crack blasted across the wall.

CCCCCCCCCCCCCCCRRRR

RRRRRRR RRRAAAAA AAAAACCCCC KKKKKKK!!!!!!!

All of a sudden Zoe could feel the whole wall giving way. Soon it all came crashing down to the floor in a blizzard of dust.

BBBBBBB

B B B B B B B C

O O O O O O O O

M M M M M M M M

| | | | | | | | | | | | | | | | | | | | | | | | |

• •

OOOOOO
OOOOOOO
MMMMM!!!!!!!!!
!!!
....

The noise was deafening, and soon all Zoe could see was white. It looked a bit like this:

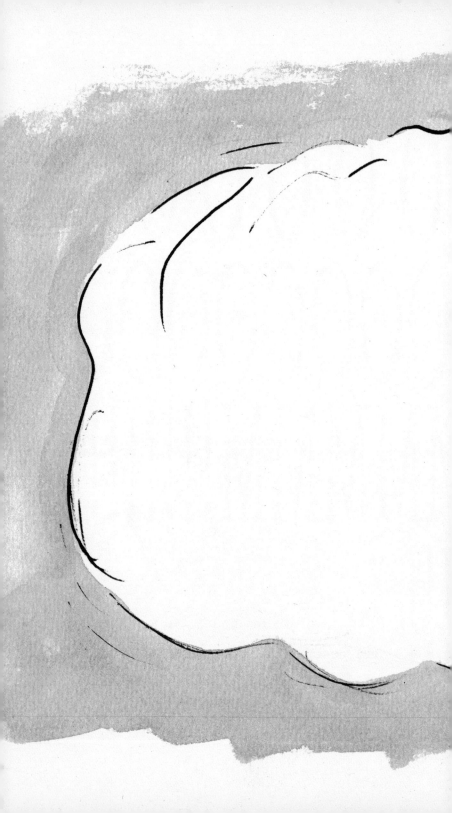

21

Sizzling Bottom

It was as if there had been an earthquake, but at least Zoe's arms and legs were now free.

Somewhere in the dust cloud in her now-shared bedroom she could hear Tina and her stepmother coughing. Zoe knew she now had a split second to make her escape, and rushed forward. Unable to see anything, she used her hands to desperately find a door handle. Zoe opened the door and hurled herself into the corridor.

Completely disorientated by the explosion of dust, it was only now she realised she was running through Tina's flat. It was even grottier than Zoe's. There was no furniture or carpet to speak of. The wallpaper was peeling off the walls and there was a smell of damp everywhere. It was as if they were living like squatters in their own flat.

However, this was no time for a makeover, even a fifteen-minute one like on TV, and after a few moments Zoe found the front door. Her little heart beating faster than ever before, she tried desperately to unlock it. Her hands were trembling, and she was unable to turn the bolt.

Then, out of the dust cloud behind her, stumbled two monstrous ghostly figures, huge and looming, all white but with open, screaming mouths and eyes bulging out red in fury. It was like something out of a horror film.

"AAAAAAAR RRRRGGGGHH!"

screamed Zoe.

Then she realised it was Tina and her stepmother, both covered head to toe in white dust.

"**AAAAAAA ARRRGGGGHH!**"

screamed Zoe.

"COME 'ERE!" shouted Sheila.

"I AM GOING TO GET YOU!" bellowed Tina.

Zoe's hands shook even more, but she just managed to open the door in time. As Zoe slid out, four chubby hands caked in white dust grabbed at her clothes, ripping strips off her blazer. Somehow Zoe managed to slip away and slammed the door behind her. Running down the communal corridor Zoe realised that both ways out of the great leaning tower block, the stairs and the lift, were sure to result in capture.

Then Zoe remembered there was scaffolding on the far side of the flats.

Thinking there might be a way down somehow, she raced over. She opened a window and climbed out on to the scaffold, before closing the window behind her. A wicked wind shook the thin boards beneath her feet. She looked down. Thirty-seven floors! Even the buses on the street looked tiny, like little toys. Zoe's head spun. This was beginning to seem like a terrible idea.

But behind her, Tina and Sheila's furious faces were pressed up against the glass, and they were banging on the window.

Without thinking, Zoe ran along the outside of the building, as her stepmother and Tina fought to be first out on to the scaffold to give chase. At the end of the wooden walkway there was a large plastic tube that went all the way down thirty-seven floors to a skip. Zoe had thought it looked like a waterslide, though it was designed to pass all the unwanted bits of debris from the building repairs down to the ground safely.

It was just big enough for a little girl.

Turning round, Zoe saw Tina and her stepmother a few paces behind her. She took a deep breath and leaped into the tube. Red plastic surrounded her, and she slid faster than she could have imagined, screaming as she went. Down, down, down. Would it never come to an end? Down and down she swirled, travelling faster and faster as she neared the ground. The little girl had never been on a waterslide, and for a moment the sensation of travelling so fast on her bottom was fun. As there was no water though, her bottom became hotter and hotter as it rubbed against the plastic.

Then, without warning, the ride finished and the little girl flew out of the tube into the skip. Fortunately there was an old mattress someone had illegally dumped in there, and it cushioned her fall. Her sizzling bottom now cooling, Zoe looked up at the scaffold.

She could see her over-sized stepmother stuck in the mouth of the tube, with Tina vigorously trying to push her down by putting all her weight on the woman's huge bum. Push and push as much as she might, Sheila's body just wouldn't fit. Zoe couldn't help but smile. She was safe, for the moment at least. But she knew someone she loved was in the most terrible danger. If she didn't find Armitage fast, he would be pulverised!

22

Free Spit

It was only when she looked at her reflection in a shop window that Zoe realised that, like Tina and Sheila, she was also covered from head to toe in dust. She had wondered why passers-by had been giving her funny looks, and why children in pushchairs burst into tears when they saw her and were wheeled by their pregnant mothers from her path.

Wiping the dust off her little plastic watch, she saw it was nearly lunchtime. Burt's van would be parked outside the school playground as it always was, frying up his noxious burgers.

The dust had gone right down the back of her throat, and Zoe was desperately in need of a drink, so she made a short pit-stop.

TING!

"Aaah! Miss Zoe!" exclaimed Raj. "Is it Halloween already?"

"Erm, no…" spluttered Zoe. "It's, er, mufti day at school, you know, where you can wear whatever you like."

Raj studied the small dusty girl. "So forgive me, but what have you dressed as?"

"Dustgirl."

"Dustgirl?"

"Yes, Dustgirl. She is a superhero, you know."

"I have never heard of her."

"She is very popular."

"Dustgirl, eh? So what is her superpower?" enquired Raj, genuinely curious.

"She is very good at dusting," replied Zoe,

now desperate for the exchange to come to an end.

"Well, I must look out for her."

"Yes, I think they are bringing out a *Dustgirl* movie next year."

"It is sure to be a blockbuster," replied Raj, clearly not a hundred per cent convinced. "People do love to watch someone doing the dusting. I know I do."

"Raj, please can I have a drink?"

"Of course, Miss Zoe. Anything for you. I have got some bottles of water there."

"Just tap water would be fine."

"No, I insist, take a bottle from the chill cabinet."

"Well, thank you."

"My pleasure," smiled Raj.

Zoe made her way from the counter and selected a small bottle of water. She downed most of it, then washed her face clean with the remainder. Instantly she felt a whole lot better.

"Thank you, Raj, you are so good to me."

"You are a very special little girl, Miss Zoe. And not just because you are ginger. Please can you pass me the empty bottle, Miss Zoe?"

Trampling dust through his little shop, Zoe returned the bottle to Raj, and he took it off behind the multicoloured plastic curtains to the back. Zoe could hear a tap running, and a few moments later he reappeared to pass the bottle back to her.

"If you could pop it back in the cabinet, please," he said with a smile.

"But it's covered in dust, and it's got my spit all around the top."

"And the beauty of the scheme, my friend, is there is no extra charge for the spit!" said Raj triumphantly.

Zoe looked at the newsagent, and then dutifully returned the bottle to where she had taken it from.

"Goodbye, Raj."

"Goodbye, er, Dustgirl. And good luck!"

TING!

Now Zoe felt a tiny little bit like she *was* a superhero, albeit one whose special power was dusting. However, just like a superhero, she was fighting evil.

Powering down the street, a trail of dust behind her, Zoe soon spotted Burt's van. It was parked where it always was outside the school playground, and there was a line of eager children queuing down the road. Approaching from the road side, she saw that the van was emblazoned with 'BURT'S PEST CONTROL'.

That's curious, she thought. Zoe hid behind the defaced and battered school sign, and waited until the bell rang for the end of lunch break. She couldn't risk being seen back at school since she was suspended. That could lead to instant expulsion.

DDDRrrrrRriiiiiiNNNNNn NNNGGGGGGGG. The bell finally rang and Burt served his final customer, squirting the peculiar dark ketchup on to the distinctly unappetising-looking burger. Zoe scuttled across the road, and hid on the other side of the van, where it faced on to the pavement. Looking up at the writing this side she saw that it read 'BURT'S BURGERS'.

"This is so strange," whispered Zoe to herself. The van said 'BURT'S BURGERS' on one side and 'BURT'S PEST CONTROL' on the other.

Zoe stared at the van. The creepy man was only using the same vehicle for catching rats that he did for frying burgers! Zoe was no expert, but was pretty sure the government's Food Standard Agency would take a very dim view of this. It was going to result in an angry letter at least.

The van's engine started, and Zoe scampered around to the back, silently opened the door and leaped inside. She closed it as quietly as she could behind her, and lay down on the cold metal floor.

Then the engine started up, and the van drove off.

With Zoe hiding inside it.

23

The Pulverisation Machine!

At eye level, Zoe could see huge bags of rotting burgers with maggots crawling out of them. She put her hand over her mouth, for fear she might scream or throw up, or both.

The van hurtled through the town. She could hear it scraping against other cars, and the horns of other vehicles hooting as it sped through red lights. Zoe popped her head up to watch in terror through a little window, as they spread chaos and carnage in their wake, not to mention quite a few broken-off wing mirrors. Burt was driving so recklessly, she was frightened he would kill them both.

The van was travelling so fast that in no time they were on the outskirts of town in a large, deserted industrial estate. Enormous empty warehouses that looked like they were falling down blotted out the sky, and soon the van stopped outside a particularly dilapidated one. Zoe looked up, out of the fat-splattered window. This warehouse was like a gigantic aircraft hangar.

Zoe took a deep breath, and everything turned dark as Burt drove the van inside. As soon as it lurched to a halt, she climbed out of the back and hid under the van. Trying to breathe as quietly as possible she looked around the giant space. There were cages and cages of rats all piled up on top of each other. It looked like there were thousands of them in here, waiting to be pulverised.

Beside the cages was a tank of cockroaches, with a sticker that simply read 'Ketchup'.

I'm so glad I never ate one of Burt's burgers, thought Zoe. Even so, she still felt really sick.

In the middle of the warehouse was a dirty old stepladder that led up to a massive machine. *This must be his pulverisation machine!* thought Zoe. It was old and rusty, and looked like it had been made out of bits from cars that had fallen apart, pieces of old freezers and microwave ovens. The whole thing was held together with sticky tape.

As Zoe watched from underneath the van, Burt approached the machine.

The main part of the contraption was a massive metal funnel, with a long conveyor belt leading from underneath it. A huge wooden rolling pin hovered over the belt. Next, metal arms that could have been parts of old food mixers stood ready at the side. On the end of the arms were round metal tubes that looked like sawn-down sections of old piping, or perhaps even parts of a lorry exhaust pipe.

If the noise of the squeaking rats was deafening, it was nothing compared to the sound of the machine.

As soon as Burt walked over and pulled the lever on the side to turn it on (which was actually an arm from a shop window dummy), the metal grinding noise easily drowned out the squeaks. The whole machine rattled as if it was about to fall to pieces.

Zoe spied on Burt as he trundled over to a cage of rats. Bending down, he picked it up – there must have been a hundred rats inside, could Armitage be one of them? – and plodded over to the stepladder, moving gingerly because of the weight. Slowly but surely he climbed up the ladder, one step at a time. At the top he paused for a moment, wobbled slightly and then smiled a sickening smile. Zoe wanted to call out to stop him, but didn't dare reveal herself.

Then Burt lifted the cage above his head and tipped the rats into the machine!

They tumbled through the air to their certain death. One little rat, not much bigger than Armitage, clung on to the cage for dear life. With a sickening laugh the evil man prised its little claws off the metal, and it plunged down and down into the machine. There was then a hideous crunching sound. He really did pulverise them! Out of the bottom of the machine poured some minced meat. The meat was then flattened by a huge wooden roller, before the arms plunged down repeatedly on to the conveyor belt and chopped the meat into patties. The patties then trundled along the belt before falling into a filthy cardboard box.

Now Zoe really did want to vomit.

Burt's terrible secret was out.

Can you guess what Burt's secret was, reader?

I should hope so: there is quite a big clue in the title of this book.

Yes. He was turning rats into burgers!

Maybe, reader, you have even eaten one yourself without even knowing…

"Noooooooooooooooo!" screamed Zoe. The little girl couldn't help it, but disastrously she had given herself away…

24

Childburger

"Ha ha ha!" said Burt, not laughing.

He paced towards Zoe, his nose twitching in her direction. Now Zoe was afraid that, like the rats, she too was in mortal danger.

"Come out, little girl!" shouted the man. "I could smell you in the van. I have an extremely strong sense of smell. For rats, but also for children!"

Zoe rolled out from under the van and ran to the door of the warehouse, which she could see even from here was shut and locked. Burt must have closed it after driving in. The cruel man walked slowly behind her. That Burt didn't bother to run made him all the more terrifying – he knew she was trapped.

Zoe looked over at the cages of rats. There must be thousands of the poor creatures stacked up in there. How on earth would she find little Armitage among them? She would just have to set them *all* free. However, right now the prodigious rat killer was striding towards her, his nose twitching more and more feverishly with every step.

Not taking her eyes off him, Zoe felt her way along the wall to the huge sliding door, and started fumbling with the padlock, desperate to escape.

"Get away from me!" she shouted, her fingers fumbling ever more frantically to open the door.

"Or what?" wheezed Burt, edging closer and closer. He was so close now she could smell him.

"Or I will tell everyone about what you are doing here. Turning rats into burgers!"

"No, you won't."

"Yes, I will."

"No, you won't."

"Yes, I will."

"Yes, you will," said Burt.

"No, I won't!"

"Ha!" said Burt. "Got you! I knew you were trouble that day in your flat. That's why I *let* you climb into the back of my van and come into my secret lair."

"You knew I was there all along?"

"Oh yes, I could smell you! And now I am going to turn you into a burger. That's what evil children get for sticking their little noses in other people's business."

"Noooooo!" Zoe screamed, still desperately trying to open the old rusty padlock. The key was still in it, but it was so stiff that, try and try as she might, it just wouldn't turn.

"Ha ha," Burt wheezed. "My very first childburger!!!"

He reached out to grab her – she dodged out of the way but his big hairy hand grasped a clump of her frizzy ginger hair. Zoe flailed her arms around, trying to get the rat catcher to release his grip. Now his other hand had slammed down on to her shoulder, and was holding it tight.

Zoe slapped him hard across the face, and his dark glasses flew into the air and on to the ground.

"NO!" shouted Burt.

Zoe looked up at his eyes, but they weren't there.

Where his eyes should be, Burt had only two empty, blacker-than-black sockets in his face.

"AAAAAAAA RRRRGGGGHH!"

screamed Zoe in terror. "You have no *eyes*?!"

"Yes, child, I am completely blind."

"But… you don't have a dog or a white stick or anything."

"Don't need them," said Burt proudly. "I've this." He tapped his nose. "This is why I am the greatest rat catcher in the world, even of all time."

Zoe stopped struggling for a moment. She was frozen in terror. "What? Why?"

"Because I have no eyes, my dear, I have developed an acute sense of smell. I can smell a rat from miles away. Especially a cute little baby one like yours."

"But… but… but… you drive a van!" spluttered Zoe. "You can't drive if you are blind!"

Burt smiled, showing off his filthy false teeth. "It is perfectly easy to drive with no eyes. I just follow my nose."

"You'll kill someone!"

"In the whole twenty-five years since I have been driving, I have only run over fifty-nine people."

"Fifty-nine?!"

"I know, it's nothing. Some I had to reverse over to finish them off, of course."

"Murderer!"

"Yes, but if you don't declare them, the insurance company lets you keep your no-claims bonus."

Zoe stared into the deep dark pools in his face. "What on earth happened to your eyes?" She knew that some people were born blind, of course, but Burt *actually had no eyes at all.*

"Many years ago, I used to work in an animal laboratory," began Burt.

"A what?" interrupted Zoe.

"Doing experiments on animals and that for medical research. But I used to stay late and do my own little experiments!"

"Like what?" asked Zoe, feeling sure the answer would be something grisly.

"Pulling wings off daddy-longlegs, stapling cats' tails to the floor, hanging bunny rabbits on a clothes line by their ears, just a bit of fun."

"Fun?"

"Yes, fun."

"You are sick."

"I know," replied Burt proudly.

"But that still doesn't explain why you have no eyes."

"Be patient, child. One night I stayed very

late at the laboratory; it was my birthday and as a special treat I had planned to dunk a rat in a bath of acid."

"No!"

"But before I could dip the little thing in the liquid, the vile creature bit my hand. Hard. The same hand I was using to hold the dish of acid. The bite made me flick up my hand in pain and the acid flew up into my eyes, burning them out of their sockets."

Zoe was speechless at the horror of it all.

"Ever since then," continued Burt, "I have pulverised every rat I could get my hands on. And now I will have to do the same to you, since you have stuck your nose into my business, like a little rat yourself."

Zoe thought for a moment. "Well," she said defiantly, "it seems to me like you got your just desserts."

"No, no, no, my dear," said Burt. "On the contrary. I am going to get my dessert just now. When I eat you!"

25

Roadkill

With one hand still on the padlock, Zoe finally managed to turn the key. She yanked her head over her shoulder and, taking her cue from the rat in the laboratory, she sank her teeth into Burt's arm as hard as she could.

"OOOOOOOOWWWWWW!!!!!!!" shouted the malevolent man, and in a reflex reaction his huge hand jumped off her tiny shoulder, yanking out a large clump of her ginger hair. Zoe flung the huge metal door of the warehouse open and ran out into the industrial estate.

The place was deserted, with sickly streetlights illuminating a wide street of empty, cracked concrete. Weeds grew out of the cracks.

Not sure of where to go, Zoe just ran. Ran and ran and ran. She was running so fast she thought she would trip over her own legs. All she thought about was putting as much distance between her and Burt as she could. The estate was so huge though, that she was still not outside of it yet.

Without daring to look back she could hear the van's engine starting up, and Burt grinding it into gear. Now Zoe was being pursued by a blind man driving a van. Finally she turned around and saw the van completely miss the open door, and crash out of the wall of the warehouse...

C C C C C C C C C C
C C C C C C C C C C C

CCCRRRRRR RRAAAAAASSSSS SSHHHHHHHH!!!!!!!!!!

The impact didn't stop it. Instead the van sped faster and faster towards her.

Squinting, Zoe could just see the dark holes where Burt's eyes had once been behind the windscreen. Just below them his nose was twitching feverishly, his smell radar clearly tuned to its 'SMALL GINGER GIRL' setting.

The van was heading straight for her and travelling faster and faster by the second. Zoe had to do something or she would be roadkill.

And fast.

She darted to the left, and the van lurched to the left too. She rushed to the right, and the van careered to the right. Behind the steering wheel, Burt's evil grin widened. He was speeding closer

and closer to making his first Small-ginger-girl-burger.

Soon, the van lurched into a high gear and started gaining on Zoe, who was running as fast as her little legs would carry her. Ahead, she spotted some bins, with a pile of long forgotten rubbish bags piled up beside them. Her mind was racing faster than her legs, and she came up with a plan...

Zoe jumped over to the bins, and picked up a particularly heavy sack. As the van hurtled towards her, she threw the bag at the bonnet of the van. As it struck, she let out a blood-curdling scream, as if she had been run over.

"AAAAARRR GGGGHHHH!!!!!!"

Burt then slammed the van into reverse, no doubt thinking he would run her over one more time to make sure she was dead.

As the engine screamed, so did Zoe. The van reversed over the sack.

Then Burt leaped out of his van, and his nose twitched as he tried to locate what he believed was the small girl's body. Meanwhile, the small girl in question tiptoed off and crawled under a wire fence into a wasteland, and kept running and didn't turn back.

After her body could run no more, Zoe jogged, and after it could jog no more, she walked. As she walked she thought long and hard about what she should do next. Zoe had witnessed a blind man who drove a van making burgers out of rats. Who would believe her? Who would help her? She *needed* someone to help her. There was no way she could take on Burt on her own.

A teacher? No. After all, she was suspended

from school and forbidden to return. The headmaster would expel her on the spot if she returned.

Raj? No. He was terrified of rats. He ran down the street in panic when he saw a baby one. There was no way she could get him to step one foot inside the warehouse, with thousands of rats inside.

The police? No. They would never believe Zoe's incredible story. She would be just another girl from the rough estate, suspended from school, and now lying to get herself out of trouble. Since Zoe was so young, the police would march her straight home to her wicked stepmother.

There was just one person who could help her right now.

Dad.

It was a long time since he had been a proper

father to her, since he had come home and given her extraordinary ice creams to taste, or played with her in the park. But Sheila was wrong, Dad did love her, he always did. He just became so sad he couldn't show it any more.

Zoe knew where to find him.

The pub.

There was a massive problem. It is against the law for children to go into pubs.

26

The Executioner & Axe

Zoe's dad went to the same boozer every day, a flat-roofed pub on the edge of the estate, with the cross of St George hanging above the door and a ferocious-looking Rottweiler tied up outside. It was not a place for little girls. Indeed, the law said that only those over sixteen were allowed inside.

Zoe was twelve. Even worse, she was small for her age, and looked younger.

'The Executioner & Axe' was the name of the pub, and it was even less welcoming than it sounded.

Carefully stepping round the Rottweiler outside, Zoe peered in through the cracked window of the pub. She saw a man who looked like her dad sitting alone, slumped over a table, a half-full pint glass in his hand. He must have simply fallen asleep in the pub. She banged on the cracked window, but he didn't budge. Zoe knocked harder this time, but Dad did not rise from his slumber.

Now, Zoe had no choice but to break the law and go in. She took a deep breath, and stood up on her tiptoes to make herself a bit taller, though there was zero chance anyone would think she was old enough to be in there.

As the door swung open, several fat bald blokes wearing England football shirts looked round, and then down to Zoe's height. The pub was barely a place for women, let alone girls.

"Get out of 'ere!" shouted the ruddy-faced

landlord. He also had a bald head, framed by some wisps of hair at the side and a ponytail. There was a tattoo on his head that said WEST HAM. Actually it didn't – it said MAH TSEW. He had obviously done it himself in front of a mirror because it was all backwards.

"No," said Zoe. "I need to get my dad."

"I don't care," barked the landlord. "Out! Out of my pub!"

"If you chuck me out I will report you to the police for allowing underage drinkers in here!"

"What the blazes do you mean? Who?"

Zoe took a sip of an old toothless man's pint from a nearby table. "Me!" she said triumphantly, before the disgusting taste of the alcohol permeated her tongue and she felt suddenly more than a little sick.

The ruddy-faced man with the ponytail was evidently quite befuddled by this logic, and fell silent for a moment. Zoe approached her dad's table.

"DAD!" she shouted. "DAD!!!"

"What? What's going on?" he said, waking up with a start.

Zoe smiled at him.

"Zoe? What on earth are you doing here? Don't tell me your mum sent you?"

"She's not my mum and no she didn't."

"So why are you here?"

"I need your help."

"With what?"

Zoe took a deep breath. "There is a man in a warehouse on the edge of town who, if we don't stop him right now, is about to turn my pet rat into a burger."

Dad looked entirely unconvinced, and pulled a face suggesting his daughter had gone more than a little loopy. "Pet rat? Burgers? Zoe, please." Dad rolled his eyes. "You're pulling my leg!"

Zoe looked her father in the eye. "Have I ever lied to you, Dad?" she said.

"Well, I, er…"

"This is important, Dad. Think. Have I ever lied to you?"

Dad thought for a moment. "Well, you did say I would find another job…"

"You will, Dad, trust me. You just have to never give up."

"I have given up," said Dad sadly.

Zoe looked at her father, so beaten by life. "You don't have to. Do you think *I* should just give up on my dream of having my own performing animal show?"

Dad frowned. "No, of course not."

"Well, let's make a deal that neither of us will forget our dreams then," said Zoe. Dad nodded uncertainly. Then she pressed the advantage. "And that's exactly why I need my rat back. I've been training him – he can do so many tricks already. He's going to be amazing."

"But… a warehouse? Burgers? It all sounds a bit far-fetched."

Zoe stared deep into her father's large sad eyes. "I am not lying to you, Dad. I promise."

"Well, no, but—" he spluttered.

"There are no buts, Dad. I need your help. Now. This man threatened to turn me into a burger."

A look of horror crossed her father's face. "What? You?"

"Yes."

"Not just the rats?"

"No."

"My little girl? Into a burger?"

Zoe nodded, slowly.

Dad rose from his chair. "The evil man. I'll make him pay for that. Now… let me just have just one more pint and then we'll go."

"No, Dad, you need to come now."

Just then Dad's phone rang. The caller's name flashed up on the screen. It read 'Dragon'.

"Who's Dragon?"

"It's your mum. I mean Sheila."

So Dad had Sheila in his phone as Dragon. Zoe smiled for the first time in ages.

Then Zoe had a horrible thought. Burt could be with her!

"Don't answer it!" she implored.

"What do you mean 'don't answer it'? I will be in so much trouble if I don't!" He pressed the answer button on his phone.

"Yes, love?" said Dad in an unconvincingly affectionate tone. "Your stepdaughter?"

The little girl shook her head violently at her dad.

"No, no, I haven't seen her…" lied Dad. Zoe breathed a sigh of relief.

"Why?" he asked.

Dad listened for a moment, and then put his hand over the receiver so what he was about to say could not be heard. "There's a pest control man there at the flat, he is looking for you. Said he is returning your pet rat to you unharmed. Wants to give it to you personally. Just to be safe."

"It's a trap," whispered Zoe. "He's the one who tried to kill me."

"If I see her, I will call you straight away, my love. Bub-bye!"

Zoe could hear her stepmother screaming on the other end of the phone as Dad ended the call.

"Dad, we need to go to his warehouse right

now. If we run we might just beat him to it, and save Armitage."

"Armitage?"

"He is my pet rat."

"Oh, right." Dad thought for a minute. "Why is he called that?"

"It's a long story. Come on, Dad, let's go. There is no time to lose…"

27

A Hole in the Fence

Zoe led her father out of the pub, round the Rottweiler and on to the street. Dad stood there swaying under the orange streetlight for a moment. He looked into his daughter's eyes. There was a long stretch of silence. Then: "I'm frightened, love," said Dad.

"I am too." Zoe reached out her hand and held her father's tenderly. It was the first time they had held hands in months, maybe years. Dad used to give her the best cuddles, but after Mum died he had retreated to the back of his eyes, and never came out any more.

"But we can do this together," said Zoe. "I know we can."

Dad looked down at his daughter's hand, so small in his, and a tear formed in his eye. Zoe smiled supportively at her dad.

"Come on…" she said.

Soon they were running through the lit streets, the intervals of dark and light going by faster and faster.

"So this nutter makes rats out of burgers?" Dad said breathlessly.

"No, Dad, it's the other way round."

"Oh yes, of course. Sorry."

"And he has this enormous warehouse on this industrial estate on the outskirts of town," panted Zoe, tugging her father along by his hand.

"That's where I used to work in the ice-cream factory!" exclaimed Dad.

"It's miles away."

"It's not. I used to take a short cut when I was late, we just need to cut through here. Follow me."

Dad took his daughter by the hand and led her through a hole in a fence. Zoe couldn't help but smile at the excitement of it all.

Then her excitement faded a bit when she realised they were entering a rubbish dump.

Soon, Dad was knee-deep and Zoe was waist-deep, wading through trash. Zoe stumbled, so Dad lifted up his daughter and put her on his shoulders like he used to when they went for a walk in the park when she was very little. His hands held her legs tight.

Together they made their way through the sea of bin bags. Soon the warehouses were in sight. A titanic graveyard of empty buildings, bathed in the harshest of light.

"That's the one I used to work at," said Dad, pointing to one of the warehouses. A beaten old sign on the side of it read 'THE DELICIOUS ICE CREAM COM ANY'.

"Comany?" asked Zoe.

"Someone's taken the 'P'!" replied Dad, and they both chuckled. "Gosh, it's been years since I have been down here," said Dad.

Zoe pointed out the warehouse that now had a van-shaped hole in the wall. "That's Burt's one!"

"Right."

"Come on. We need to save Armitage."

Father and daughter skirted around the outside edge towards the giant hole in the wall. They stepped inside, and peered at the cavernous warehouse. The huge building appeared empty, except for the thousands of rats. The poor creatures were all still piled up in cages, awaiting their grisly fate as a fast-food snack.

Burt was nowhere to be seen – he must still be at the flat with Zoe's wicked stepmother, waiting to trap Zoe when she came home. No doubt salivating at the idea of turning her into a burger, albeit a particularly large one.

With trepidation, Zoe and Dad stepped inside, and Zoe showed her father the terrifying pulverisation machine.

"He goes up this ladder and drops the rats into this giant funnel, and the poor little things are rolled flat here before being formed into patties."

"Oh my word!" said Dad. "So it *is* true."

"What did I tell you?" replied Zoe.

"Which one of these poor little blighters is Armitage?" asked Dad, gazing at the thousands of terrified rodents squashed high into the mountain of cages.

"I don't know," she said, scouring all the little frightened faces, peering out from the cages, which had been stacked on top of each other. Seeing them all there, squashed in together in a big tower of rats, made her think of the block she and Dad and Sheila lived in.

Still, thought Zoe. *The rats had it worse. What with the getting minced up into burgers.*

"Now where is he?" she said. "He's got a very cute little pink nose."

"Sorry, love, they all look the same to me," said Dad, desperately trying to spot one with a particularly pink nose.

"Armitage? ARMITAGE!" called Zoe.

All the rats eeked. Every single one of them wanted to escape.

"We'll just have to set them all free," said Zoe.

"Good plan," replied Dad. "Right, you climb on my shoulders, and unlock the top one."

Dad lifted his little daughter up and sat her on his shoulders. She then held on to his head, and slowly stood up.

Zoe started unwinding the pieces of metal

wire that kept the cages locked. I say cages –
they were really old deep-fat fryers.

"How are you getting on?" said Dad.

"I'm trying, Dad, nearly got the first one
open."

"Good girl!" called up Dad encouragingly.

However, before Zoe could open the first cage, Burt's van, looking decidedly the worse for wear, came thundering into the warehouse, smashing the huge metal sliding door into the air as it did so...

CCCCRRRRR
RRAAAAAASSSSSSSS
SSHHHHHHHH!!!!!!!!!!!

...before screeching to a halt.

RRRRRRRRRRRRRR
RRRRRRRRRRRRR
RRRRRRRRRRRRR
RRRRRRRRRRRRRR
RRRRRRRRRRRRR
RRRRRRRRRRRRR
RRRRRRRRRRRRRR
RRRRRRRRRRRRR

!!!!!!!!!!!!!!!!!!!!!!!!!!!!!!!
!!!!!!!!!!!!!!!!!!!!!!!

Dad and Zoe were in deep deep trouble...

28

Rat Poison

"Now I've got you!" wheezed Burt, as he leaped down from the driving seat. "Who's that with you, little girl?"

Dad looked up at his daughter nervously. "No one!" he said.

"It's me useless git of a husband!" announced Sheila, as she plopped down from the other side of the van.

"Sheila?" said Dad, aghast. "What are you doing here?"

"I didn't want to tell you, Dad," said Zoe, stepping down from her father's shoulders to the ground. "But I heard him and Sheila being all lovey-dovey…!"

"No!" said Dad.

Sheila smiled smugly at the pair. "Yeah, the little weasel's right. I am goin' to run away wiv Burt in 'is van."

The woman strutted over to the rat catcher, and took his hand. "We share a deep love of each other."

"And pulverising rats," added Burt.

"Oh yeah, we love to kill a rodent or two!"

With that the pair shared a stomach-churning kiss. It was enough to make Zoe want to hurl.

"I fancied ya more with the moustache though, Burt," said the stupendously thick woman. "Will you grow it back?"

"You two are disgusting!" shouted Dad. "How could you enjoy killing all those poor creatures!"

"Oh, shut yer face, ya idiot!" hollered Sheila. "Those rats deserve to die, disgustin' little fings!" Then she paused for a moment and looked at her stepdaughter. "That's why I murdered your 'amster."

"You killed Gingernut?" screamed Zoe, tears in her eyes. "I knew it!"

"You evil cow!" shouted Dad.

Sheila and Burt shared a sickening laugh, united by cruelty.

"Yes, I didn't want that dirty little fing in me flat. So I mixed some rat poison in wiv his food. Ha ha!" added the repulsive woman.

"How could you do that?" shouted Dad.

"Oh, shut ya face. It was only an 'amster. I always 'ated it!" replied Sheila.

"Rat poison. Mmm. A nice lingering death!" added Burt with a breathy laugh. "They just taste a bit funny afterwards, is all."

Zoe hurled herself at the pair – she wanted to tear them both to pieces. Dad pulled her back.

"Zoe, no! You don't know what they'll do." Dad had to use all his strength to stop his daughter from attacking them. "Look, we don't want any trouble," he pleaded. "Just hand over my Zoe's pet rat. Now. And we'll go."

"Never!" wheezed Burt. "The baby ones are the most succulent. I was saving him for our little date, Sheila. Mmm…"

Slowly, Burt reached towards the filthy pocket of his apron.

"In fact," he said, "I have your precious Armitage right here…"

Then he pulled the little rat out by the tail. Zoe's pet rat had been in there all along, and not in the cages after all! Burt had tied Armitage's little hands and feet tightly together with metal wire so he could not escape. He looked like a little rat escapologist.

"Nooooo!" shouted Zoe when she saw him like that.

"He is going to make a very tasty little burger!" said Burt, licking his lips.

Sheila studied the poor little thing dangling in the air, and then turned to Burt. "Ya can eat him, my one true love," she said. "I might just stick to the prawn cocktail crisps, if ya don't mind."

"Whatever you like, my angel sent from heaven."

The blind man stumbled towards the pulverisation machine, and turned the lever. A terrible grinding sound echoed through the warehouse. Slowly Burt began to climb the stepladder to the top of the funnel.

"Put down that rat!" shouted Dad.

"As if anyone ever paid the least bit of attention to ya! You're a joke!" laughed Sheila.

Zoe struggled free of her father's grip, and ran after Burt. She had to save Armitage! However, by this time the malevolent man was halfway up the stepladder, and poor little Armitage was wriggling his little body as much as he could and squeaking in terror. Zoe grabbed at Burt's leg, but he shook his foot violently to shake her off. Burt then kicked her in the nose with the heel of his boot. She was knocked down hard on to the concrete floor below.

"**A A A A A A A H H H H H H H H ! ! ! ! ! ! ! ! ! ! ! !**" screamed Zoe.

Dad sprinted over to the ladder and pursued the rat killer up on to it. Soon the two men were standing precariously on the top step, the ladder swaying side to side under their combined weight. Dad grabbed Burt's wrist, and pushed it down to force him to release his grip on the little rat.

"Drop me husband in the burger machine while you're at it!" jeered Sheila.

Dad's elbow brushed up against Burt's face and knocked the rat catcher's glasses off his head. Coming face to face with the dark pools where the man's eyes should have been, Dad was so horrified he stepped back and lost his footing. His foot slipped backwards off the top of the stepladder towards the funnel.

He began to slide down into the pulverisation machine. Dad desperately grabbed on to Burt's apron for survival, but it was so greasy he was instantly losing his grip.

"Please please," said Dad. "Help me up."

"No. I am going to feed you to the children," rasped Burt, his laugh rattling around his throat, prising Dad's fingers one by one off his apron.

"And your daughter is next!"

"Yeah! Throw her in as well!" cheered on Sheila.

Badly winded, Zoe rose unsteadily to her hands and feet, and crawled over to the stepladder to help her father. Sheila desperately tried to stop her, grabbing the little girl brutally by the hair and yanking her back. Then she swung her stepdaughter around by the hair and flung her into the air.

Up, up, up…

And then down.

Hard.

Zoe screamed in agony as she hit the ground for the second time.

"Aaaaaaaaah hhhhhhhhhhhhhhh!!!!!!!!!!!!!"

Despite her thick frizzy hair, the impact dazed Zoe for a moment.

"Burt? Stay there and I'll 'elp ya finish 'im off!" called Sheila to the two men still fighting over the top of the burger machine. Slowly, the grotesquely large lady made her way up the steps, the ladder creaking under her considerable weight.

Still dizzy, Zoe opened her eyes, to see her stepmother wobbling at the top of the ladder. The woman was trying to prise Dad's fingers off Burt's greasy apron. One by one she was bending them back, laughing as she forced her husband closer and closer to being turned into a burger.

However, Sheila was so heavy that as she bent to one side to prise off the poor man's final little finger, her weight made the whole ladder topple over to the side.

CCCCRRRRRA AAAAAASSSSSSSSSSSS HHHHHHHHHH!!!!!!

Burt and Sheila fell forwards, headfirst into the pulverisation machine...

...Dad just managed to grab on to the side of the funnel with one hand...

...Armitage was falling into the machine with the cruel rat catcher. Nothing could stop the baby rat being pulverised...

29

Pink Furry Slippers

Just then, as Burt tumbled through the air, Armitage bit the monster's finger and, squealing, Burt flicked the rat off his hand and up into the air.

Up, up, up…

…and into Dad's outstretched hand.

"Got him!" called Dad. Now he was hanging on by one hand to the lip of the funnel, and clutching Armitage with the other. Armitage was squeaking like crazy.

At that moment there was a gurgling sound and the gruesome twosome passed through the machine.

It clunked and groaned like never before, as they passed through the rollers. Finally two very large burgers trundled out.

In one, Burt's shattered wraparound shades poked out. In another, Sheila's pink furry slippers were clearly visible. They were two distinctly unappetising-looking burgers.

"HELP!"

yelled Dad. He was
moments from being a
burger himself...

Zoe's attention shot
back to the funnel.

Her father was still
holding on to the side of
the pulverisation machine
with one greasy hand,
gripping Armitage in the
other.

Dad's feet were still dangling over the grinders below, scuffing the tips of his shoes with a noise like a piece of paper being lowered into a desk fan.

Zoe could see that he was sliding. The grease on his hand from Burt's apron meant that slowly but surely he was losing his grip.

Any moment now, he was going to breathe his last breath.

And then come out of the machine as another rather large burger.

Her head still spinning from its collision with the floor, Zoe crawled over the cold wet concrete floor of the warehouse to the machine.

"Turn it off!" shouted Dad.

Zoe rushed over to the lever on the side. But try as she might, she couldn't get it to budge.

"It's stuck!" she called up.

"Grab the ladder, then!" called Dad.

Zoe looked: the stepladder was lying on its side on the ground where it had fallen.

"QUICK!" shouted Dad.

"EEK!" shouted Armitage, wrapping his little tail as tight as he could round Dad's free hand.

"OK, OK, I'm coming!" said Zoe.

With all her strength, the little girl righted the ladder, and ran up the steps. At the top she peered down into the huge machine. It was like looking down into the mouth of a monster. The metal grinders were like giant teeth that would chomp you to bits.

"Here!" said Dad. "Take Armitage."

Zoe reached down to take the little rat from her father's hand. Dad passed Armitage up, his legs and feet still bound together by metal wire. She hugged him close to her chest, and kissed him on the nose. "Armitage? Armitage?

Are you all right?"

Dad looked up at this moving reunion and rolled his eyes.

"Never mind about him. What about me?" he yelled.

"Oh, yes, sorry, Dad!" said Zoe. She put Armitage into her inside breast pocket and then crouched down on the ladder and offered her hands to help pull her father out. However, Dad was heavy and Zoe wobbled precariously at the top of the ladder, nearly falling headfirst into the machine.

"Careful, Zoe!" said Dad. "I don't want to drag you in too!"

Zoe took a couple of steps back down the ladder, and curled her feet around a step to form an anchor. Then she reached out her arms, and Dad held on to them, and finally pulled himself up to safety.

After climbing down the ladder, Dad yanked on the lever, turned off the machine, and lay exhausted on the floor.

"Are you OK, Dad?" asked Zoe, standing over him.

"A few cuts and bruises," he said, "but I will live. Come here. Your old dad needs a cuddle. I do love you, you know…"

"I always knew, and I love you too…"

Zoe lay down next to her father, and he put his long arms around her. As he did so, she took Armitage out of her pocket, and carefully untied his legs. Together, they had a big family cuddle.

Just then Armitage interrupted. "Eek eek!" he said, before doing a little dance to draw Zoe's gaze up – up to the tower of rats still squashed so cruelly into cages.

"I think Armitage is trying to tell us something, Dad."

"What?"

"I think he wants us to set his friends free."

Dad looked up at the towering wall of cages, which all but reached the ceiling of the warehouse. Every cage was squashed full of poor starving rats. "Yes, of course. I quite forgot!"

Dad moved the ladder over to the cages, then stood on top of it, and with Armitage safely back in her pocket, Zoe climbed on to his shoulders to reach the top cage.

"Steady!" said Dad.

"Make sure you hold on to my feet!"

"Don't worry, I've got you!"

Finally, Zoe managed to open the first of the cages. The rats clambered out as fast as they could, then used the little girl and her dad as a ladder to climb down to the safety of the ground. Soon Zoe had opened all the cages and thousands of rats were running excitedly around the warehouse floor, enjoying their new-found freedom. Then Zoe and her dad broke open the tank of cockroaches, which had narrowly escaped being ground into 'ketchup'!

"Look," said Dad. "Or, actually, don't look. You're too young to see this."

Of course, as you must know, reader, there is nothing more guaranteed to make a child look than this.

Sure enough, Zoe looked.

It was the freshly made Burt and Sheila burgers. The rats were devouring them greedily and finally having their revenge!

"Oh dear," said Zoe.

"At least they are getting rid of the evidence," said Dad. "Now come on, we'd better get out of here…"

Dad took his daughter's hand, and led her out of the warehouse. Zoe looked back at the battered van.

"What about the burger van? Burt won't need it any more," she said.

"Yes, but what on earth are we going to do with it?" asked Dad, looking at his daughter quizzically.

"Well," said Zoe. "I have an idea…"

30

Room-mates

Winter turned to spring, as the van was redecorated. Just removing the grease that had built up on every surface of the vehicle, inside and outside, took a week. Even the steering wheel was thick with slime. However, the work didn't seem like work, because Zoe and her dad did most of it together, and it was surprisingly fun. Because he was so happy, Dad didn't go to the pub once, and that made Zoe happy too.

There was a snag of course; being unemployed, Dad only received a small amount of benefit money. It was a pittance and was barely enough to feed him and his daughter, let alone refurbish a van.

Fortunately, Dad was an ingenious sort.

He had found lots of the bits and pieces he needed for the van from the rubbish dump. He rescued an old discarded little freezer and repaired it. He used that to keep the lollies cold in. An old sink was just the right size to fit in the back of the van for rinsing the scoops. Zoe found an old funnel from a skip, which with a bit of paint and papier mâché, the father and daughter managed to fashion into an ice-cream cone to stick on the front of the van.

And so it was finally done.

Their very own ice-cream van.

Zoe's suspension from school was being lifted tomorrow. However, there was still one final decision. One major, crucial thing they had to make their minds up about. One really important outstanding matter.

What to write on the side of the van.

"You should name it after you," said Zoe, as they stepped back to admire their handiwork. The van stood gleaming in the afternoon sun in the car park of the estate. Dad held a brush and a pot of paint in his hand.

"No, I have a better idea," he said with a smile. Dad lifted his hand up to the side of the van and started painting on the letters. Zoe looked on, intrigued.

'A' was the first letter.

"Dad, what are you writing?" asked Zoe impatiently.

"Shush," replied her father. "You'll see."

Then 'R', and then 'M'.

Soon Zoe had it too, and couldn't resist shouting out. "*Armitage!*"

"Yes, ha ha!" laughed Dad. "Armitage's Ices."

"I love it!" said Zoe, jumping up and down on the pavement with excitement.

Dad added the 'I', then the 'T', then the 'A', 'G', 'E', the apostrophe, because everyone knows apostrophes are very important, then the 'S', and then the word 'ICES'.

"Are you sure you want to name it after him?" asked Zoe. "He is just a little rat, after all."

"I know, but without him, none of this would ever have happened."

"You're right, Dad. He is a very special little fellow."

"You never did tell me why you called him Armitage, by the way," said Dad.

Zoe gulped. This was absolutely not the time to tell her father he had written the name of a toilet on the side of his gleaming ice-cream van.

"Er... it's a long story, Dad."

"I've got all day."

"Right. Well, another day. I promise. In fact I had better just go and get him. I want him to see what we have done to the van..."

Armitage was all grown up now, and didn't fit in her blazer pocket any more. So Zoe had left him in the flat.

Zoe excitedly ran up the stairs of the tower block, and rushed into her bedroom. Armitage was scuttling around Gingernut's old cage. Dad had liberated the cage from the pawn shop by exchanging it for a bumper box of prawn cocktail crisps his ex-wife had amazingly left uneaten.

Of course, the room wasn't just Zoe's bedroom any more.

No: since the wall had fallen down it was now a room twice the size that she shared with someone else.

That someone else being Tina Trotts.

The council were meant to have repaired the wall ages ago, but it was still down. To Zoe's surprise, when she entered the room, Tina was kneeling beside the cage and tenderly feeding the little rat little crusts of bread through the bars.

"What are you doing?" asked Zoe.

"Oh, I thought he might be a little peckish…" said Tina. "I hope you don't mind."

"I will take over, thank you," replied Zoe, snatching the food out of Tina's hand. She was still suspicious of everything the big girl did. After all, Tina was the one who flobbed on Zoe's hair every day on the way to school. The misery she had caused would not be easily forgotten.

"Do you still not trust me?" asked Tina.

Zoe thought for a moment. "Let's just hope the council gets that wall up soon," she said, eventually.

"I don't mind," said Tina. "I have enjoyed sharing a room with you, actually."

Zoe said nothing. The silence hung in the air for a moment, and Tina started to fidget.

Aargh, thought Zoe. *Stop feeling sorry for Tina Trotts!*

The thing was, though, that in the past few weeks Zoe had come to understand a lot more about Tina's life. How her horrible father screamed at her most nights. Tina's father was a great bear of a man. He enjoyed making his daughter feel worthless, and more and more Zoe was wondering if that was why Tina did the same to others. Not just to Zoe, but to *anyone* weaker than her. A great grinding wheel of cruelty, that could go round and round for ever if someone didn't stop it.

Yet as much as Zoe now understood Tina, she still didn't like the girl.

"There is something I need to say to you, Zoe," said Tina suddenly, her eyes filling with tears. "Something I've never said to anyone. Ever. Ever ever ever. And if you repeat it, I'll kill you."

Goodness, thought Zoe. *What on earth could*

it be? Is it some terrible secret? Does Tina have a second head that she keeps hidden under her jumper? Or is she really a boy called Bob?

But no, reader. It was none of these things.

It was something much more shocking…

31

Rich and Famous Rat

"Sorry," said Tina, eventually.

"Sorry? That's the thing you've never told anyone, ever?"

"Er… yes."

"Oh," said Zoe. "Oh, OK."

"Oh, OK, you forgive me?"

Zoe looked at the big girl. She sighed. "Yes, Tina. I forgive you," she said.

"I am *so* sorry for being so cruel to you," said Tina. "I just… I get so angry. Especially when my dad's… you know. It just makes me want to squash something small."

"Like me."

"I know, I am so so sorry." Tina was actually crying now. It was making Zoe a bit uncomfortable – she almost wished Tina would flob on her instead. Zoe put her arms around the girl, and hugged her tightly.

"I know. I know," said the little girl softly. "All our lives are hard in one way or another. But listen to me…" Zoe rubbed away Tina's tears tenderly with her thumbs. "We need to be kind to each other, and stick together, OK? This place is tough enough without you making my life a misery."

"So no more flobbing on your head?" said Tina.

"No."

"Not even on Tuesdays?"

"Not even on Tuesdays."

Tina smiled. "OK."

Zoe passed the crusts of bread back to Tina. "I don't mind you feeding my little boy. Carry on."

"Thank you," said Tina. "Have you taught him any new tricks?" she asked, her face brightening in anticipation.

"Take him out of his cage and I'll show you," said Zoe.

Tina gently opened the door to the cage, and Armitage tentatively crawled on to her hand. This time he didn't bite her: instead he nuzzled his soft fur against her fingers.

Zoe took a peanut from a bag on the shelf, as her new friend gently lifted Armitage out on to the still dust-encrusted carpet. She showed him the peanut.

Armitage promptly stood on his hind legs and did a very entertaining backwards dance, before Zoe gave him the nut. He took the nut between his paws and nibbled at it greedily.

Tina started applauding wildly. "That's amazing!" she said.

"That's nothing!" replied Zoe, proudly. "Watch this!"

With the promise of a few more peanuts, Armitage did a forward roll, a back-flip, even spun around on his back as if he was breakdancing!

Tina couldn't believe her eyes.

"You should take him on that TV talent show," said Tina.

"I would love to!" said Zoe. "He could be the world's very first rich and famous rat. And you could be my assistant."

"Me?!" asked Tina, incredulous.

"Yes, you, in fact I need your help with a new trick I have been dreaming up."

"Well, well, I'd love to!" spluttered Tina. Then

she said, "Oh!" as if she had just remembered something.

"What is it?" said Zoe.

"The end-of-term talent show!"

Zoe still hadn't been back at school since her three-week suspension started, so she had completely forgotten about the show.

"Oh, yes, the one Miss Midge is organising."

"Midget, yes. We should totally enter Armitage."

"She is *never* going to allow me to bring Armitage back into school. He was the whole reason I got chucked out in the first place!"

"No, no, no, they talked about it in assembly. As it is in the evenin', the 'eadmaster has made a special rule. Pets are allowed."

"Well, he's not a dog or a cat, but I suppose he is my pet," reasoned Zoe.

"Of course he is! And get this. Midget plays

the tuba, I heard her practisin'. It's awful! All the kids reckon she is only doin' it because she wants to get off wiv the 'eadmaster."

"She so fancies him!" said Zoe.

The two girls laughed. The idea of the unusually small teacher playing the unusually large instrument already seemed hilarious, let alone using the low-noted tuba as a method of seduction!

"I have to see her do that!" said Zoe.

"Me too," laughed Tina.

"I just need to show Armitage something downstairs quickly, then we can spend this evening working together on the new trick!"

"I can't wait!" replied Tina, excitedly.

32

Actually Too Much Fudge

Running down the stairs was easier than going up, and before the paint was dry on the side of the van, Zoe was breathlessly showing Armitage the results of her and her father's hard work. Dad climbed into the van and opened the sliding hatch. Zoe had never seen her father looking so happy.

"Right, so, you're my first customer. What would you like, Madam?"

"Mmm…" Zoe surveyed the flavours. It was a very long time since she had tasted the delicious frozen dessert – she wasn't even sure if she'd ever had ice cream since those evenings when her dad would rush home from the factory with some crazy new flavour for her to try.

"Cone or cup, Madam?" asked Dad, already relishing his new job.

"Cone, please," replied Zoe.

"Any particular flavour take your fancy?" asked Dad with a smile.

Zoe leaned over the counter and studied the long line of mouth-watering flavours. After all those years in the factory, Dad really did know how to make some truly scrumptious ice cream. There was:

Triple Chocolate Sundae
Strawberry & Hazelnut Swirl
Fudge, Fudge & more Fudge
Toffee Popcorn Explosion
Caramel & Honeycomb Crunch

Fudgetastic Surprise

Tutti-Frutti-Lutti

Raspberry Ripple with Dark Chocolate Chunks

Double Fudge & Coconut Cream

Cookie & Caramel Crunch

Fudge, Fudge, Fudge & more Fudge

Toffee & Peanut Butter Swirl

Pistachio & White Chocolate

Banoffi Pie with Mega Fudge Chunks

Butterscotch Bonbon Boom

Marshmallow Milkshake Supreme

Quadruple Choc Chip with Honey Swirls

Mini Chocolate Eggs & Fruits of the Forest

Snail & Broccoli

Fudge, Fudge, Fudge, Fudge, Fudge, Fudge,
Fudge, actually now too much Fudge.

It was the most magnificent collection of ice-cream flavours in the world. Apart from the

Snail and Broccoli, obviously.

"Mmm… They all look delicious, Dad. It's just too hard to make a decision…"

Father peered down at his array of ice creams. "Then I will just have to give you one of each then!"

"OK," said Zoe. "But maybe leave out the snail and broccoli?"

Her dad bowed. "As you wish, Madam."

As his daughter giggled, he piled up her cone with flavour after flavour until it was nearly as tall as she was. With Armitage in one hand, she balanced the impossibly tall ice-cream cone in the other.

"I can't eat all this on my own!" laughed Zoe. She looked up at the tower block, and saw Tina looking down at her from the 37th floor window.

"TINA! COME DOWN!" shouted Zoe at

the very top of her voice.

Soon lots of children were poking their faces out of the windows of their flats, wondering what all the noise was about.

"ALL OF YOU!" shouted Zoe up at them. She recognised a few of them, but most of them she didn't know. Some of them she had never seen before in her life, even though they were all so closely crammed into this huge ugly leaning building together. "Come on down, everyone, and help me finish my ice cream."

Within seconds, hundreds of kids with dirty but eager little faces were rushing down to the car park to take their turn to have a bite of Zoe's ridiculously tall ice cream. After a few moments, the little girl entrusted the tower of ice cream to Tina, who made sure all the kids received their fair share, especially

the tiny ones whose little mouths couldn't reach that high.

As the sound of laughter rose and the sun went down, smiling Zoe broke away from the laughing children and sat alone on a nearby wall. She brushed the litter off the wall and brought Armitage up to her face. Then she gave him a tender little kiss on the top of his head.

"Thank you," she whispered to him. "I love you."

Armitage tilted his head and looked up at her, with the sweetest little smile on his face. "Eek eek eeek eeeeeek," he said. Which, of course, from rat to English translates as:

"Thank you. I love you too."

Epilogue

"Thank you, Miss Midget, I mean Midge, for that beautiful tuba playing," lied Mr Grave. It had been truly awful. Like a hippopotamus farting.

Miss Midge tottered off the stage at the school talent show, unseen behind her huge, heavy instrument.

"That way, Miss Midge," called Mr Grave, in a concerned voice.

"Thank you, headmaster," came a muffled voice, just before Miss Midge crashed into the wings. The tuba sounded better hitting the wall than when she had played it.

"I'm all right!" called Miss Midge from beneath her ridiculously large tuba.

"Er… right," said Mr Grave.

"Might need the kiss of life though!"

Mr Grave, impossibly, went even more pale. "Next," he said, ignoring the teacher struggling beneath her ridiculous brass instrument, "please welcome the final act to the stage – Zoe!"

There was a cough from the side of the stage.

Mr Grave looked down at his sheet of paper. "Oh, um, Zoe and Tina!"

The audience all applauded, none louder than Dad, who was sitting proudly in the front row. Raj was sat next to him, clapping excitedly.

Zoe and Tina ran on, in matching tracksuits, and took a bow. Then Tina lay down on the stage, as Zoe set up what looked like little ramps either side, which they had made from cereal boxes.

"Ladies and gentlemen, boys and girls, please welcome: 'The Amazing Armitage'!" said the little ginger girl.

At that moment, Armitage sped across the stage, riding a wind-up toy motorbike that Dad had bought from a charity shop and repaired, and wearing a tiny crash helmet.

The crowd went wild just at the sight of him, apart from Raj, who covered his eyes in fear. He was still scared of rodents.

"You can do it, Armitage," whispered Zoe. When they had practised, he had sometimes missed the ramp and just drove past it, which didn't make for a very exciting show.

Armitage whizzed faster and faster as he reached the ramp.

Come on, come on, come on, thought Zoe.

The little rat hit the ramp perfectly.

Yes!

Armitage took off —

Armitage flew through the air —

Oh no! thought Zoe.

He was coming down too soon. He was going to miss the ramp on the other side.

Down, down, down Armitage fell—

Zoe held her breath—

And then he landed on Tina's ample tummy.

Bounced back up in the air.

And landed on the ramp on the other side.

It was a moment of pure and utter joy. It probably even looked deliberate.

"Oof," said Tina.

"Eek," said Armitage, bringing his motorbike to a perfect stop.

The audience instantly rose to their feet and gave them a standing ovation that went on for ages – Raj even peeked out from behind his hands.

Zoe looked at Armitage, then Tina, then her dad, who was clapping like a mad man.

She couldn't help but smile.